The Raising of

Leonard Lamply Jr.

John M. Davidson

NFB
<<<>>>
Buffalo, NY

NFB
119 Dorchester Road
Buffalo, NY 14213

For more information visit
Nofrillsbuffalo.com

INTRODUCTION

There are plenty of ways to raise a child. There are several people that need to be involved to set a little one on the right path. Oh sure, there are relatives; mom, dad, aunts, uncles and the like, but it takes a lot more influences to bring up a youth. Teachers, clergy, babysitters, neighbors, even politicians. When it comes to children there can be no shortage of bodies around.

These are the people that shape a child. They are the ones who are charged with what the child will ultimately turn out be. Each person who has had contact with said child is responsible, in some way, for their life. Of course at some point, around eighteen, it is determined that this child is an adult. However, at this point the child is already formed. He or she is off into adulthood with all that was taught to them by the main characters and the role players from their childhood.

I suppose that one could wonder what would happen if those people were not around. Or worse, what if they were a composition of losers, sluggards, ill equips, and your general ner'-do-wells. It is often said that it takes an entire village to raise a child.

Personally, I think it takes an entire village to screw one up.

ZERO

January 23, 1978

"My daughter is here to deliver the baby."

"And which one's your daughter?"

"The one right over there moaning in pain with the unborn child. I hardly think that I need to point her out; she is the only woman in the waiting room."

"I'm not blind, or deaf for that matter. What is her name?"

I feel a bit ruffled by the tone, but I don't think it is time to bicker on about manners. "Kingston, Martha Kingston." I try to sound full of calm.

"We'll have her in right away; she sounds like she's ready to pop." She says this like she's some kind of balloon or a starting cap.

"They'll have you in momentarily," I say as I take a seat next to Martha. I am still trying to be supportive. I can try to be unconditionally supportive on this one day. After this one day I tell you my support is coming with conditions, lots of conditions. After all, Walter and I are going to be raising this little one; the writing is already on the wall.

"I can't go in now mah!" She says this to me like she has some kind of say in the matter.

"Well what on earth are you going to do, sit out here until you deliver because you're afraid to release this baby into the world?" The calm is starting to give way.

"I don't mean I can't ever go in there! I need'ta wait on Lenny!"

"That bum is probably drunk on the floor or drunk in your sister's bed," the calm has all but left the body. "Either way he's drunk and not coming here for the birth of the little one. I say we are better off for it!" The last part was meant to be in my head.

"How can you say that, and how can my child be better off born with no him here?"

Thank goodness the nurse is here with the chair. This will give me an opportunity to reclaim my calm. I am wondering how all this has happened as we are making our way to the delivery room. I feel that Walter and I have done all there is to do to raise a bright and elegant daughter in this world. I find myself, as usual, coming to the same conclusion. That child Walter brought with him. She is nothing but trouble. She has infected my sweet Martha with that trouble!

"Well is it you or is the mister on his way?"

My train of thought was interrupted and I am confused. "Is I what, rather, am I what?"

"Coming in? You or the father? Or is she to go at this alone?"

I feel like this is an accusation rather than a question. "I will be with my daughter; it seems the father is tied up at the moment." I try to sound convincing, trying to sound as if I still have the calm.

As they are moving Martha to the bed I find myself again trying to locate the moment when everything went sour for my sweet Martha. Was it in the third grade when she lost Patrick the class rabbit? She cried and cried. I suppose we could have purchased her a new one and saved her the difficulty of having to arrive at school the following Monday Patrick-less. She must have been devastated by her classmate's reactions. She cried at the breakfast table that entire week.

"Mah! Will you please help me out here?" I am snapped out of the memory of her tears into the reality of her tears, accompanied by grunts and moans. I take her hand and tell her she is doing fine. However, I think she is over doing it a bit. She really knows how to ham it up. Hopefully she will feel better after the drugs.

"I think it's time for the epidural." I say this trying

to mask my discomfort at the sound of my daughter's tears with the voice of a concerned mother.

"No, no drugs!"

"Excuse me?" I am not sure who said this first, the nurse or me. Although, I don't feel it is within her right to make comment and I shoot her a look just so that she knows this.

"No drugs. Leonard and I decided that we don't want our baby all drugged up and stupid when it comes out."

"I can see that you wouldn't want your little one to come out acting like that bum but Leonard is not here to help with this decision and I am," calm gone again, "and I think that you should take the epidural to ease the pain that you are going to be coming into rather shortly." She seems to be ready to say something when another contraction comes. It must be a doozy because she confirms to the nurse through clenched teeth that it is, in fact, time for the epidural.

I feel briefly relieved that she has taken my advice on the epidural matter. However, almost immediately behind that thought is the realization that the pain made the choice, not my advice.

If that less than loser Leonard were here he would have told her no shot, and she would have listened. She sure would have listened to him. He would have said "No shot for her!" and probably tried to procure some drugs for himself. He would have got them too. He would have concocted some story about anxiety of the baby's arrival or something to calm his nerves about the delivery room, would he have. He can be quite convincing, some people say. I have seen it work on others myself. But not me. No, not me.

I knew that he was trouble the moment Leonard Lamply walked into the room on the first day that he came to take my sweet Martha out. He only came to the door because Walter wouldn't let her out of the house when he honked that silly horn on that obnoxious truck of his.

With his greasy hair and his mustache. Oh, that mustache. Dirty, little, wiskery, weak, mustache. His eyes were half closed and glossed over, like he had been smoking drugs or drinking beer. I knew right away that he was no good trouble. Walter said that all boys try to grow hair on their face as soon as there is a trace of ability, but I don't see boys like that down at the church. No you see boys like that on the news at eleven o'clock.

Did I trust my gut? No. We let her go out with that loser Leonard that very night. We have regretted it ever since. The way she fawned over that boy for the last three years has been nothing short of pathetic. Doesn't listen to a word I say, or her father for that matter. Why can't she see it? As I start to ponder why she can't see what a no good loser this Leonard of hers really is, I feel extreme pain in my hand.

"Mah! What the hell, would you please say something!" She is screaming this at me like she has already asked me a question, although I don't believe that she has.

"I'll say this, no matter how much pain you're in I don't appreciate your use of language. Just think of how much it would hurt if you didn't take that shot; if you'd have listened to Leonard." I can only imagine the language she would be using then. She never used to use language like that.

"Just talk to me, I gotta get my mind off this pain and try to hold it in until Lenny gets here."

"I think you may have to accept that Leonard may not make it." I feel sick that I can't find anything else to talk about with my daughter other than her boyfriend who is not here for the birth of their child. Unmarried and having her first baby. Eighteen years old and having a baby. No good father to be not here, probably not even aware that she is at the hospital. We haven't had anything to talk about in years. Just arguments over curfews and Leonard, unholy language and Leonard, beer and Leonard, sex and Leonard!

"Thanks, Mah, you always know just what to say."

"I'm sorry dear," although I'm not. "I'm not quite sure what to say. I planned on this day being further away from your eighteenth birthday." I have lost all of the calm and support, with or without conditions.

"Oh great, a gilt trip! Now mah? A guilt trip now? You know that's why Lenny isn't here. He isn't here because of you and the way that you talk to him and treat him. You're always judging him and talking to him like he's a moron. I don't blame him for not being here, I don't blame him at all!"

"Him not being here has nothing to do with me. It has to do with him and his decision to be with other losers, or your sister, or both!" I am reeling and wishing for a piece of that calm, just a small portion of it, back.

"AHHH, can you make her leave?" She is screaming to what appears to be no one in particular, which is probably why no one replies.

"I'm not leaving, I love you and I am sorry that I upset you with what I have said." I am sorry that I have upset her. I am not sorry about anything that I have said about that bum. I am only sorry that I could not keep calm for the birth of her baby. This is not how I had planned this all to go. I was going to be her rock. I was going to win her back and show her that even though Leonard was no good and not going to be around, that I would be.

"Fine, fine, you can stay." She says this like it was actually in question.

"Well, does it feel like a girl or a boy?" After I ask this I begin to wonder myself. Strangely, I realize that I haven't given this much thought. One would think being a grandma to be for the first time I would be daydreaming about a little girl to have a tea party with, or a little boy to dress like a cowboy. You would think I would picture sitting with a child on my lap to read to, and you would figure in this fantasy the child listening to the story would be a boy or a girl, not just a faceless, genderless, doll like you win at some county fair. In my defense this whole affair hasn't been exactly a daydream, or anything close to a fantasy, for that matter. No, quite the contrary. This has been much closer to a nightmare or at least a nine-month uneasy realization. A realization that Walter and I are not even close to being finished as parents, a realization that our lives will be put on hold, again, to raise another child.

"What do you think?" I realize that Martha has already answered and I have missed it.

"As long as it is a healthy child I will be pleased." I hope that I am not transparent. "Do you have any names picked out?" This should give me an idea of what her previous answer was.

"I always liked the name Missy."

"Melissa? Like your friend from the swim team?"

"The swim team? Mah, I haven't been on the swim team in years, let alone talked to her. And no, not like her at all. Missy, not Melissa." I don't care for the attitude that she uses in the word Melissa but I let it go because I am still afraid that she may realize that I was not paying attention earlier.

"You can't name her Missy. Missy is not a real name. It's a nickname for a girl named Melissa." It's also a bit whorish if you ask me, but no one did and I am hoping to take this opportunity to find some of that calm that I had so diligently prepared to bring with me.

"I can name her whatever I want; she's going to be my daughter. Besides, Lenny likes the name Missy."

Oh I bet he does. I don't say this, of course, but why wouldn't that cad of a man like a whorish name like Missy. He probably had himself a trampy little thing named Missy before he was with my Martha. The more I think about it I am willing to bet that he has had himself a Missy while he was with my Martha, may even be with her right now. Rather than take this opportunity to point out what a lowlife this Leonard of hers is I ask a question to divert the Missy discussion, "Well, what if you have a boy?" I can almost feel a tinge of calm working its way back into my demeanor.

"I dunno mah, it's feeling like a girl."

"Well feelings can always be wrong."

"Not mine mah, my feelings are almost always spot on."

She's really upsetting the renewed demeanor. None the less I try to remain in a discussion, rather than an arguing, tone. "Well dear what if you do have a boy some day," goodness I hope it's not soon that she will be having another one of these, "what will you name him?"

Before she has a chance to answer a portly fellow in blue scrubs walks into the room. He looks a little out of shape to be a doctor. You would think that a doctor, someone who is responsible for so many other people's well being and health, would be in better shape.

"Hello mom, and mom to be." He directs his introduction, first, to me and then to Martha. His voice somehow matches his out of shape figure. "My name is Doctor Abbott," now focusing on Martha. "I am going to just take a peek here and see what's what."

"I think I'm ready doc."

"Well then let's take that look," he says with a goofy smile. The man, his voice, and his smile all match in the same foolish looking, and sounding, way. I really should have helped Martha find a good gynecologist. It's a rather personal thing, but perhaps I really should have helped.

However, I was tremendously busy helping Walter fix up the basement. How can I be expected to help convert the basement into a fit visiting room for the baby and find a good doctor? I shouldn't have to do everything! I have already raised my child; she's eighteen and needs to be more responsible for her own life.

"I think your right mom to be." I wonder if he even knows her name. "Alright mom," or mine for that matter, "We're going to need you to hold her hand and remind her to breath. I think we are just a few minutes from having a baby."

"Okay honey, you can do this. Just breathe and listen to the doctor." Here is my opening. I am going to be the cornerstone for her. Helping her breath, keeping her calm, holding her hand, reminding her to push at the big moment, this is my chance. Maybe when this is all over and we are sitting together with her new baby she will realize that I was here the whole time, helping her through this difficult moment. Leonard gallivanting off who knows where? All the while I, her mother, was right by her side, here to help.

"Okay, big push," the doctor says cuing me.

"Okay sweetie big push." I say this in a powerful way that makes it my own, not just regurgitation from the inane doctor. She is squeezing my hand uncomfortably hard but I am not going to say anything right now unless it is helpful.

After a few more go rounds on the pushing the doctor announces, "Okay we have a head, let's have one more big push."

"You're doing great Martha, one more big push should do it."

I'm going to spare you all of the messy details and let you know that, after a short labor, Martha and our family was presented with a baby boy. The nurse brought him into our room after they had cleaned him all up. She handed him to Martha and headed back for the door. She stopped short and said, "I'll be back in a few moments with some papers to fill out," then left us to ourselves.

So here we are, looking at this beautiful baby boy. He's beautiful. He looks like Walter. "How amazing is it that he looks just like your father." I am ecstatic at our good fortune.

"I dunno mah, I think he looks a lot like Lenny. His eyes are green like Lenny's. He looks cute, like Lenny too."

She says this to hurt me, I can feel it. His eyes are green, and so are Leonard's, but they aren't the same. Leonard's eyes are set deep in his head and look beady and up to no good. This little baby boy, in the spitting image of Walter, has full lovely eyes. Nothing like his father's, except for the color.

"You know mah, I think that once Lenny meets his son it will help him settle down a little bit. Did dad settle down once he saw me?"

"Your dad was never wild. Beyond that he was responsible and present for your birth, not off sowing wild oats all over Buffalo." I feel myself getting riled up but I try to force it away and change the subject. "Anyway that was then, let's enjoy this moment here with your gorgeous son."

"He is good looking, isn't he?"

"That he is."

"I should stop calling him 'him' and 'he' and give him his name."

"On account of his good looks and all that he has done for you, and undoubtedly will be doing for you, I think a fine fitting name would be Walter. Walter Kingston." Just as I am finishing the sentence the nurse bursts in with such a racket that I'm not even sure that Martha heard my name suggestion.

"Okay I will let you two spend some more time with your special boy on your special day right after we give the special one a name." She directs this at Martha, ignoring me almost all together.

Martha looks sure of herself as she tells the nurse what name to put on the birth certificate. "Leonard."

I am stunned, "Leonard? No, no, Leonard Kingston doesn't even have a ring to it. It doesn't sound proper."

"You are right." She says this to me while looking at the nurse.

"So what will it be then?" The nurse seems exasperated as she inquires.

Martha has a wry smile "Leonard Lamply. Leonard Lamply Jr."

ONE

February 4, 1979

"I don't know where he is mah! He doesn't have to check in with me, I trust him." I don't really trust him but it's none of her damn business where the hell he is. Even if he is out getting drunk again while his fiancée and baby are up all night worrying about his sorry ass. Even if he did promise to come home early and spend time with his son, only a single year old. I worry that little Lenny won't even know who is father is at this point, with how little he gets to see him. So no, I don't know where he is but that doesn't mean she should come down here prying into the matter.

"Well he shouldn't have to check in, I agree with you there. He shouldn't have to check in because he should be in, taking care of you and his son. It's the least he could do. He doesn't work and he doesn't pay us a lick of rent to stay in our basement." Here she goes again. "I mean what kind of man doesn't want to step up and support his family? Or at least get them out of his girlfriend's parent's basement?"

"I don't know mah? He is trying his best. He looks for a job every day but it's hard out there right now. No one is hiring. And I'm his fiancée not his girlfriend." No one will hire someone who shows up drunk asking for applications. If he even is asking for applications. There is a good bet that he is just out wandering the streets of South Buffalo looking for drinks and pills. He hasn't come home in any shape in weeks, if he comes home at all.

"Well your father and I are getting pretty sick of him stumbling around here and not lifting so much as a finger to help you or your son. If he isn't going to work he could at least offer to help Walter around the house. It isn't easy for him to work all day and then come home and see Leonard, as useless as he is, doing nothing. Doing nothing, living in our basement, doing nothing. A fine man you have chosen to be the father of your son. And he isn't your fiancée. You don't have a ring on. No ring, no wedding plans, he doesn't even come home every night."

"Okay mah, I appreciate your little pep talk. I have to feed little Lenny now and we would appreciate a little peace and quiet." I say this as coldly as I can with the intent that she will get the hell outta here and go back upstairs to bother my dad.

"Fine, I'll be going upstairs now."

"Great, and I'll let you know the next time I need your advice."

"You live here in my house and my house comes with advice. If you don't like the advice then you and your wonderful Leonard can find your own place, but I won't be expecting that any time soon." The volume of her voice but not the intensity trails off as she heads back upstairs, to the rest of the house.

Right then I realize that I, too, need to go upstairs to get the formula from the fridge. That damn formula that Lenny doesn't even like. No matter, soon he will be eating baby food. I wanted to breast feed, but Lenny had me drinking within a day of being home from the hospital. I suppose I could have objected a little more forcefully. I suppose I could have just said no, like those stupid advertisements say. Like it's that easy; I have news for the unrealistic advertisement company pushing those signs down our throats: it's not. Try saying no to a drunken fiancée who just wants to get drunk and if you don't get drunk with him he will walk out that very door which you walked in with your first born, only a day earlier. Put that on one of your retarded signs at the bus stop.

No point in dwelling in the past. I just hope that nosy rag isn't up there waiting for me to come get Lenny's formula. I always hate going upstairs. It's only eleven steps with a railing but it feels like a whole 'nother world. At the fourth or fifth step I can usually predict whether the coast will be all clear and by the seventh I can be fairly certain one way or the other. Tonight it seems like some movement around the fourth step and by the seventh I am sure that there is someone in the kitchen.

"Hey sweetie."

Thank goodness, it's my dad. He is a big, sweet man. His size isn't intimidating. I think that it is because his big size is offset by his even bigger glasses. You see, he wears these coke bottle sized bifocals. I don't believe that anyone could be too intimidating in those. I often wonder how the other iron workers take him serious in those. I suppose when you are the boss you can wear whatever you want and be taken serious.

What about when he wasn't the boss? How did he make it to being the boss with those on his face? I suppose these are questions I will save for a time when he is not preparing for bed. I don't think I could ever ask my father those questions with a straight face anyway.

Aside from his large outline and coke bottle glasses he looks like any other dad from Buffalo. He looks tired and a little weathered; you can see it in his rough, leathery face and graying hair. Even his thick mustache has wisps of grey in it. But he is a sweet man. He has maintained his sweetness no matter how my mother tries to nag it out of him. He treats her with respect in spite of how much she shits on him, both in private and in public.

"Hi daddy. I am just here to grab the formula from the fridge."

"I don't think your mother has mixed any up."

"What! She knows what time it is. I guess I'll just do it myself. This is just like her. To punish Lenny because she is mad at me. I can't stand her!"

"Sweetie, she seemed pretty upset just now when she came up from the basement. She probably just forgot, I don't think it was intentional."

I want to respond but I hear the side door open slowly. I also hear what I believe to be four separate attempts to close the door.

"It sounds like Leonard is home. Please ask him to be more careful when he parks his car. He left tire tracks on the edge of the lawn again."

"I will daddy. He was talking about getting outside and helping you with the lawn this week." I don't like lying to my dad but I hope that he believes me and passes that message along to my mother. It seems like a silly lie since the lawn is still covered with a light layer of dirty snow and road salt from the cold winter. I suppose if the lawn is a concern for my father in February then maybe the lie is believable.

"I'll be in my room if you need anything sweetie."

"Thanks, I am just going to mix up some formula and head downstairs to see how Leonard's day was." I am already thinking about pouring myself a glass of wine while hugging my father before he heads to bed. I used to feel a bit guilty about finishing the night with a glass of wine before bed. That was before I was used to going to bed alone every night. Each night worrying about Lenny. Where is he? What is he doing? Finally, and most nervously, with whom is he with? All these worries are eased a little with a small to moderate sized glass of wine. Of course, on a real dinger of a night the worry can only be subsided with a hearty glass full.

I commence to poor myself a full glass of wine before starting the formula. Once I finish the formula I fill the empty half of the wine glass before putting the wine away. Before heading downstairs I remember to also put the formula away. I don't want to hear her voice first thing in the morning complaining about the order of the kitchen.

The converse of the fear of heading up the stairs is the joy of heading down those same stairs. Joy to be moving in the opposite direction of my mother and in the direction of my little Lenny. This evening that joy is muddled because I am all too sure that Big Lenny is as drunk as a skunk, or worse. I am not familiar with any other animal analogies about being drunk but Lenny usually gets as drunk as an elephant.

"Hey baby. Let me have a sip of that wine."

There he is. Father holding son. Drunk as an elephant. Shirtless.

"No." I am the one who deserves a relaxing drink.

"Yeah right. Give me that glass."

His beady eyes are fixated on my glass. He seems pretty steady on his feet, although I can tell he is heavily intoxicated.

"No, my parents don't want you drinking in the house."

"They don't want either of us drinking in the house. If you can, then I can too."

"That isn't how it works. I am having a relaxing glass of wine before I feed Lenny and go to bed." Relaxing my ass. This is the only thing that helps me sleep after such a long day alone with Lenny. All he does is cry and piss. He is like a sniper with that little thing of his, always hitting my clothes or his clothes. At least when he hits his clothes he can spend the rest of the day naked. I have to either change or smell like piss the rest of the damn day.

"Well let me relax with you. Then we can relax together."

He has that look in his eye. That look when he is drunk enough to want to have sex and sober enough to actually do it.

"Where did you park?"

"Don't worry I parked on the street because tomorrow your parents need to leave before I do."

"Of course they do because they have jobs. Maybe tomorrow after you finally come to you can go and find one yourself. By the way, be careful to not drive on the lawn anymore. My parents are pissed about that."

"The lawn? It's fucking February, there is snow everywhere! Who gives a shit if I catch the corner of the lawn?"

"My dad, the guy who let's us live here, that's who gives a shit." I'll stick up for Lenny to my mother but I'll stick up for my dad to Lenny. Lenny always gets pissed about my relationship with my dad and I enjoy it. I relish any time this topic comes up as it usually ends with Lenny feeling like dog shit.

"Screw your dad. He's always in our shit. Too bad he is so passive or he could just tell me what he really thinks and not pass me notes through you. Your dad acts like he's in the fourth fucking grade."

"He's not passive, he's polite. Anyway could you either put on a shirt or put down little Lenny. I don't want him absorbing all the boozy sweat on your skin."

"I'll tell you what. I'll trade you our little Len here for your glass of wine. I'll hold it for you while you feed little Len. How's that for a deal?"

"Whatever, just put him down." Normally I would love to see Lenny holding our son but not tonight. Not when he is covered in nasty sweat, and rickety like a drunken pachyderm.

Lenny puts him down and then heads toward me for what I am assuming is my glass of wine; it's still a little early for him to make a move on me. I immediately take the biggest swallow my throat will allow because I am sure I won't be getting that glass back until it is time to be washed. As I am swallowing I almost choke. The wine has nothing to do with it. It's Lenny. He stinks like cheap perfume again.

"Alright leave something for the man of this house."

"Man of this basement," I correct him, "and you're hardly even that."

"Excuse me! What in the hell does that mean?" He snags the glass away from me on the conclusion of those words.

"It means you aren't man of this home because we live in a basement and furthermore," now I'm really rolling, "you are barely man of this basement because you are hardly ever around. And why did you take off your shirt?"

"What?"

"Your shirt? Why did you take it off so quickly after you got home?"

"I spilled a drink on it and it was wet."

"I don't believe you." Although I do believe him. I believe that he spilled a drink on his shirt. That is wholly believable. However, I don't believe that is the reason that he took it off.

"It's over there in the dirty pile. You can see the stain from here."

"I know you spilled your drink. You are a sloppy, no good, drunk. I don't believe that is why you took it off! Your pants are filthy, and there they are still clinging to your legs," I am growing wild with anger, "but your shirt is over in the dirty pile."

"Oh really. And why do you think I took it off then? And be careful the way you talk to me."

"Don't make me say it you dirt bag!"

"Careful now with that tone. You're getting pretty feisty. You might wake your daddy and he might have to send your mommy down."

I knew the bit about my father earlier had gotten to him.

"You scum bag. You spent another night with that

whore!"

"Which whore are you referring to, there's just so many?"

"You cold, awful man. You realize you are in front of your son, talking to his mother like that." I am through with him. He is always drunk and never working. He is always horny and doesn't care who satisfies him, even if it is my own skanky half sister. I hate that slut. I don't know how my dad could also have that bitch. He must not know either, that's why he sent her ass packing years ago.

"Some mother he has. A drunken hag who can't even please her own man. Why do you think I get so many women? I'll tell you why, because I'm a king in the sack and you're a wet blanket who doesn't even moan when she excites."

"Get out! Get the hell out of here! I never want to see you again. Go. Go now!"

"It would be my pleasure."

With that he simply turns around and leaves. Just like that. He doesn't put down the glass or put on a shirt. Just leaves.

As I sit down it starts to dawn on me what has happened. The father of my son has left. I have never told him to leave before. I don't know how this will play out from here. I am pretty sure that he is gone for good.

Although it will be impossible to never see him again in this town. However, I am fairly certain that this is the last we will be seeing him around here. I feel a sense of freedom. It isn't as if I have truly lost anything. He provided nothing financially or otherwise. Little Lenny and I still have the same roof over our head. Unfortunately our roof is my mother's floor.

As soon as I think of little Lenny in my father's basement I realize...Damn it! Little Lenny, I forgot to feed him. I better do it now and hope that he doesn't realize the difference in our schedule. That would be just like his father to make a general disturbance and then leave me with the aftermath. Of course, this is a bit more than the general disturbance. My thoughts are interrupted by Lenny's tears of hunger.

I can barely get my thoughts together before I hear the basement door open and my mother's shrill voice.

TWO

April 6, 1980

"Oh, I never complain about an order being too big Mr. O'Malley." And that's true. I could never complain to a customer about his spending money at Nowak's.

"No I suppose you haven't, have you Ron." Is it my imagination or is he actually contemplating this declaration.

I can't imagine a time that he could be thinking of. I always try to stay upbeat and positive, especially at the store. That's the way my father did it over sixty years ago when he opened the store and, by golly, that's the way I promised him I would do it when I took over almost nineteen years ago now.

"Well just in case I have, I tell ya what I'm gonna do for you," he'll love this. Everyone loves a good deal, "I am going to knock off five cents a pound on this here roast beef. That's what I am going to do for you Mr. O'Malley."

"Oh, Ron you don't have to do that for an old rambler like me. I was just talking; you have never been anything other than polite and pleased to help the people of this neighborhood."

"Well I guess I'll just make it three cents per pound." I hope my smile is big enough for him to know it's a joke and of course I'll be knocking off the original five cents per pound.

"All right, all right, what's the damage going to be today Ron?"

"That will be $6.43 Mr. O'Malley." I know Mr. O'Malley is getting up there in years but I am sure that his math is still accurate enough to see the discount in the total bill.

As he hands me a ten he says, "Thanks a lot, Ron."

And as I make change I say, "It's been my pleasure Mr. O'Malley." Then, as I hand him the change I add, "Come again," brief pause, "real soon."

Small talk. Yes, that's what makes this place so special. That's what makes this place better than any of the chain convenient stores or super gas stations. No, people come to Nowak's because they can count on a little personal chatter. I can't say that I blame them either. As I lose myself in thoughts of all things Nowak's I hear the door chime signaling another customer looking for a little personal attention. Almost simultaneously I feel a minute tightness that grabs my body as I recognize my customers.

"Why, hello Martha." Okay Ronald, I tell myself, hold it together. Her mother is a fine woman and pays all her bills on time. She is a mother just trying to raise her little boy. It must be tough as a single mom in South Buffalo, you over hear the way people talk about her. "And hello to you Leonard, what can I do you for today folks?"

"Hey Mr. Nowak, I just came up here to grab a few things for little Lenny and me to have at the apartment."

"How is having your own place? I bet little Leonard here is enjoying his own bedroom." I wonder if she knows that Mrs. Kingston has already told me that she has moved out of the basement and into her own place. I hope that I don't seem forward asking her about a situation that she has not yet told me about personally.

"We are both enjoying that." She says this as much to Leonard as she does to me. I feel relieved that my already knowing is not an issue. Of course, she must know that I know because her mother had already made an arrangement to allow her to buy on credit and then Mr. Kingston will be in later to pay the bill himself.

"Well grab a basket and start shopping I'll be over here looking for a special treat to give Leonard if he is a helpful shopper to his mom." I started the whole treat thing after a few occasions where he was not being so helpful to anyone. The last instance was when I found him alone in isle three chewing on a bag of marshmallows. He managed to chew through the plastic and by the time I found him he looked like he had rabies with all that mallow on his face. His mother did not seem very upset when I informed her of the situation. Mrs. Kingston didn't find it so amusing when I told her. I felt a little two faced telling her mother, but I have a store to run and can't have children chewing up all of the products and knocking items off of the shelves while he runs free.

Either way things have gotten much better since I started keeping a few treats off to the side for when Leonard is here with his mother. Nothing too extravagant, usually a couple of chocolate Tootsie Rolls or a butterscotch to enjoy. I keep them next to the register and hold them until the very end. That has really been doing the trick these past couple of months.

"Hey Mr. Nowak we are all done. On your way over here could you grab me a pack of smokes? Any kind you want, just make sure they are filtered. I don't want Lenny here to accidentally inhale any of the chemicals."

I don't even begin to tell her how second-hand smoking works. "Sorry Martha, your mother was very specific about not allowing cigarettes on her tab."

"Oh really, is there anything else I should know about when choosing options to feed my son and me?"

"No, no restrictions on items for feeding."

"Okay Ron I get it. What are the other restrictions on not feed foods?"

I don't care for her tone and I can't imagine it will be improving when she hears this, "No alcohol or rolling papers, in addition to the tobacco products." I must admit I felt a little joy in telling her this. I also feel a little sullen having to explain these rules to such a young mother who should know. Mothers should just already know these things.

"Well, Mr. Nowak, how much are the cigarettes going to cost me?"

"They are $.85 Martha."

"Okay, I'll be right back with your money. Watch Lenny for a minute would ya."

This is clearly not a question. "Hold On," I have to act quickly because Martha is already heading for the door and last time she left Lenny here it was a debacle, "Where are you going?"

"I'm just going around the corner to my friend's house. He will loan me a buck. I don't have any money on me and my apartment is nine blocks away. I'll be right back."

"Now Martha, last time you said that you didn't come back for nearly an hour."

"Mr. Nowak I give you my word I will be right back. Besides, Lenny really likes you. He always looks forward to coming up to Nowak's so he can see Mr. Ron Nowak in person. You're a regular celebrity to him."

"Martha I need you back here right away. I have a business to run and can't be watching Lenny for you."

"Right back, Mr. Nowak, I promise." With that she dashes out the door.

Okay Ron we can handle this. He's just a little boy, can't be much past his second birthday. This time we just need to stay on top of him and not let him go roaming all over the store. That Mrs. Kingston is not going to like hearing about this. I suppose if Martha gets right back here I won't go telling her anything. What can I have this little fella working on for me? I have just the idea.

"Leonard my friend, do you want to help me count these boxes over here?" No response.

"Leonard. I asked if you would like to help me count all these big old boxes over here with me. It could be fun." This time Leonard stands up from the floor and waddles over.

"Okay buddy, glad to see you made it over. Now how high can you count?" He stares at me but doesn't answer.

"Can you count to 10?" Nothing. "How about 5?"

Nothing. "Can you count at all?" This isn't going so well. But it has been a couple of minutes. Martha should be back any second. Last time she didn't. I better come up with something quickly.

"Mr. Nowak?"

That voice sure isn't Martha's. "Oh, hello Mr. Murray. Sorry, I didn't even hear you come in. I was so busy counting boxes over here with Leonard."

"Is that so? How many boxes did the two of you count so far?"

"We hadn't really got to counting yet, still just warming up. To be honest Leonard doesn't really seem to be one for counting."

"Mr. Murray, you have a whole mess of boys don't you?"

"I see what you're getting at there Ron and my boys are no younger than twenty two these days. Hell, one of my boys has a boy all his own."

"I'm just going to ask for advice Mr. Murray. I'm not going to ask you to take him home. His mother has been gone for about ten minutes, should be back any minute. Just ran across the street to grab some money to pay for her bill."

"She should have taken that boy of hers with her, if you ask me."

"Oh come on now Mr. Murray, the only thing I was going to ask you is if you have any ideas on how to keep this little one busy a couple more minutes?" Maybe more.

"Well the first thing you need to do is locate the boy."

I wheel around to see nothing but the boxes. I spin around the other way and find no signs of Leonard. I do catch a smirk on Mr. Murray's face. Not an entire smile, just enough of one to know that he thinks he could do better. Frankly, I'm sure that he could. I had myself two girls and neither one is anything less than sweet.

"Come on Ron, let's look for him. It's a nice store but it isn't very big. You start over there and I'll start over here. We'll meet in the middle and one of us will have the boy by then."

With that he heads his way and I have no choice but to head mine. I glance at my watch and it has been nearly fifteen minutes now. How could that be? Is my watch broken? Was the conversation with Mr. Murray's longer than I assumed? We didn't even count any boxes yet?

Martha should be back any minute. I hope we have him found by then. Well, maybe I don't. It wouldn't be so bad for her to see what happens when she leaves her son here and doesn't come back for chunks of time. I told her last time I would be calling her mother if she pulled this again. I am thinking of actually doing it too. I am Ron Nowak and I run a convenient store not a daycare.

While I am trying to come up with something to say to Mrs. Kingston I hear the sound of breaking glass. Almost simultaneously I turn the corner and find Leonard trying to pick up another thirty two ounce juice bottle in addition to the broken one lying next to him in pieces.

"Leonard put that down!" I hear the booming voice of Mr. Murray. No wonder his boys were always so well behaved in my store. To say that his voice is thunderous and intimidating would be underselling it a great deal.

"Be careful you guys that's broken glass." I am hoping that no one slips in the juice and falls on the glass. What a mess that could make. I already have to clean up juice; I don't want to spend the afternoon scrubbing blood from the isle. I hate the smell of bleach.

"Alright Mr. Nowak you take care of the spill and I will take care of the boy."

I immediately feel nervous. Mr. Murray didn't sound like he was going to watch over Leonard. No, the way he said 'take care of' had an entirely different meaning than I would like. As I head off to get the mop I hear Mr. Murray really hollering at Leonard. I was in the middle of telling myself that it could be exactly what that boy needs when I hear a crash again. This time it is not the sound of a juice bottle hitting the floor. No this is more like the sound of a hand crashing into a child. There it is again, followed by more thunder. Just as I can stand no more I hear him order Leonard to go sit down by the counter. Thank goodness, because if that had kept up I might have had to say something to Mr. Murray.

I try not to make eye contact with Mr. Murray as I head past him to the spill.

"Mr. Nowak I am going to be taking one of these newspapers. My wife will be in later in the week to pay the bill."

"Absolutely Mr. Murray, your wife is always quick with payments. Tell her I look forward to seeing her later on in the week."

"I'll pass along the message. The boy shouldn't be giving you anymore trouble."

Then I hear the door chimes signaling that Mr. Murray has left. The only sound now is the stifled cry of a little boy. I try to ignore the sounds as I finish cleaning up. I look at my watch and realize that another ten minutes has passed by, putting us at nearly thirty minutes. One half hour! That's it I am going to have to call Mrs. Kingston. It is her right to know what is going on with the welfare of her grandson.

I am making my way toward the phone behind the

counter when I catch a glimpse of poor Leonard. He is covered in snot and tears. He looks so dour. Maybe I can wait five more minutes.

"Leonard do you want that treat now?" I am met with more silence. Now, I know that this boy can speak. I have heard him in here speaking with his mother and his grandmother. I am fairly certain he's even been in here gabbing with his grandfather. If he won't answer then I won't be giving him any treat. Stubborn little boy.

I am at this moment reminded how pleased I was to have a pair of beautiful little girls. Oh sure it would have been nice to have a son to pass Nowak's on to. But if this is the price I would have to pay just to hand down my store that my father had handed down to me, then no thank you. I'll give Leonard one more try, and I'll be giving Martha just one more minute.

"Leonard it's time for your treat. What would you like?"

Muffled cry.

"Would you like a hand full of tootsie rolls or a piece of butterscotch?"

One solitary sniff.

"Okay, Leonard because you have been sitting so politely since Mr. Murray left I will offer you a popsicle. Just this one time though."

Silence.

"Okay Leonard then you will be receiving no treat this week. I hope that next week you won't be so stubborn. And where is your mother?"

I'm not really expecting him to answer but it has been over half an hour since she was dashing across the street for a dollar. I should have just given her the cigarettes and told her mother she purchased $.85 worth of salami. Now I am stuck in a fine predicament. I am here watching a mute child who either is breaking my things or being broken himself by my customers. This is a convenience store! What is going on here! This is it! I am going to call his grandmother and let her sort this all out.

"Leonard I am going to call grandma and see if she can come and pick you up until your mom is finished with her errands. Do you want me to tell her anything?" I don't even pause to see if he will answer on my way to the phone.

As I am looking through my address book for Mrs. Kingston's number I start to feel nervous. What am I going to say? What am I going to do if Martha shows up while I am on the phone? I put the book back down and head to the parking lot.

I look as far as I can see in each direction. There is no sign of Martha. But what if she arrives in a car? Okay I will stand here and wait until I see no pedestrians that could be Martha and no oncoming cars that could possibly contain Martha. This takes a few minutes but my nerves are settled by the end of this. On my way back in the store my eyes are immediately drawn to two things. First the clock; it has been nearly forty minutes. The next are Leonard's blue dashed lips.

"Leonard did you take one of my popsicles?"

What a surprise, I am met with silence. I don't see the wrapper or the popsicle stick anywhere but it is clear that Leonard has taken, and eaten, the popsicle. Well that does it. I am going to be calling Mrs. Kingston this instant!

This time I do not hesitate to open the little address book with the red leather cover, pick up the phone, and dial.

I am met by Mrs. Kingston's voice, "Hello. Kingston residence, how may I help you?"

"Hello Mrs. Kingston. It's Ron Nowak, down at Nowak's." I try to sound pleasant yet firm.

"Mr. Nowak. Well what can I do for you?"

"Well it's about Martha."

"I am sure that she has really rung up a tab. It was her first time there since moving into the apartment so I am sure that in the future it will be less expensive. I give you my word that Walter will be down there to pay the bill inside this week."

"Oh I don't worry about the bill. You are always

good for it."

"Well then what seems to be the problem Ron?"

"Well now Mrs. Kingston, I have Leonard here again."

THREE

December 28, 1981

"You got a light, I can't find mine?" I know she does. She always has at least one, and usually a couple of lighters on her.

"Yeah sure, can we come in first? It's freezing out here."

"He can come in," I move out of the doorway to let Len Len in, "you can find me a light." I know she's stalling so she can try and get in my house. She wants to snoop around for signs of Lenny.

"Okay, let me find one. I know I have one in one of these pockets."

"Well hurry up, my shows are about to come on." Still stalling.

It's times like these that I just can't understand why our spineless father let her bitch of a mother kick me out. If they could see their precious little Martha now they would spin back the hands of time and toss her ass out and give me my own room. Look at her. All strung out. She can't even afford a babysitter while she goes across town to pick up her welfare check and food stamps. She can't bring Len Len with her because she'll want to stop on the way home to cop her shit. Hell, she can't even find a fucking lighter in all her cluttered pockets.

"Here you go, but I need it back." She looks agonized at the thought that I won't give it back.

"All I need to do is light this cigarette and then you can be sure that I will give it back and close my door. Listen you better not be gone for days again. I don't have enough food and shit for him to stay here longer than a couple hours."

"I'm just running downtown and I'll be back by three." She doesn't even pause before extending, "Four at the latest. Can I please have that lighter back?"

"Hold your horses; I haven't even lit the fucking thing yet. You think I'm going to steal it or something?"

"It wouldn't be the first time you stole something from me."

"Oh Martha, you have quite the imagination."

"Look I need to get going to catch the bus, could you just light your smoke and give me back my damn lighter?"

"Shit!" The flame is nearly a foot high from this

little lighter. That's typical of a junkie loser.

"Sorry, I don't know how that happened."

"It probably happened when you were getting high."

"You know what, screw you. Just give me back the damn thing and go watch your crummy shows."

"Poor little bitch."

With that final exchange I toss her lighter just over her left shoulder and shut my door. That was a little too long of a conversation with dear Martha anyway. Besides my shows are starting.

"Len Len what are you watching?"

"Fun House Aunt Aileen. It's time for the alphabet song. Do you want to sing it with me?"

"What? No. I already know the alphabet. Change it to channel two. My shows are going to start."

"Can I watch them too?"

"Sure Len Len just be quiet until the commercials. I'll grab us a couple drinks. What do you want?" He better say cola or water because those are the only options he has, unless he wants Vodka.

"Root beer."

"I ain't got any root beer. I'll get you a cola. I'll grab one too."

As I look through the fridge I can't find the pop.

There isn't anywhere for it to hide because I haven't gotten to the store recently. I find it on the counter with the top off. I know that Lenny must have left it there because it's right next to the vodka, also with the lid off. I'll just have to add some ice. As I turn around I realize that Lenny probably used all of the ice up too. Sure enough there are only three cubes left in the tray. I suppose it's three more than I expected. I pour two glasses of pop and drop the ice into my glass. Since it is already open I also pour in some of the vodka.

I don't bother putting anything away because I hear my shows starting and head quickly to the couch.

"Move over Len Len so I can sit too. This is my couch."

"My pop is warm. Can I have some ice?"

"No, there isn't any left."

"Not fair."

"Well, you can thank your father when you see him. He should be coming over in an hour or so." Ever since he turned three he has been a real pain in my ass. He seems to talk more and he definitely whines a lot more.

"Mommy told me not to see daddy."

"Well your mommy isn't here and she probably won't be for awhile. Besides you can't tell her that your dad was here anyway. Got it?"

"Why?"

"Because I said so. Now shut up and turn up the volume." The benefit to having Len Len here is that he can get up and change the channel or adjust the volume for me. Damn batteries.

Len Len turns up the TV and we spend some time watching our shows when all of a sudden I feel like if I don't make it to the bathroom in the next ten seconds I am going to explode. It's an awful pain from my stomach to my head. Even as I am running to the bathroom I am not sure if I am going to shit or vomit. I suppose I'll know soon enough.

As it turns out I do neither. Both the stomach and the bowels are calm as soon as I lock the bathroom door. However, I do catch a glimpse of myself in the mirror. Not exactly a princess today. I am contemplating washing my face and brushing my teeth before I abruptly realize that I am missing my shows. I head back towards the living room after rinsing out my mouth with some warm water.

"Blech! Aunt Aileen your pop is bad."

"Damn it Len! That isn't for you. I poured you your own drink. Stay the hell away from mine." It's then that I realize that his glass isn't even empty, "Why the hell are you drinking mine anyway? Your glass is still half full."

"Mine's warm. I just wanted a sip sip."

"Well then take another sip sip and leave mine alone after that." Maybe if he gets a little of that in him he will fall asleep like the last time.

"No, it's bad."

"Just try one more sip. It gets better each sip."

"No. It's bad."

"Fine. Now shut up and let's watch our shows." All of these interruptions are keeping me from my soap. This one has really been heating up lately. All kinds of drama. However, it's nothing compared to the next show, but it does get you in the mood for it.

We spend the next several minutes wrapped up in the show. I love trying to figure out what happens next. I am very good at it. I suppose it is because I am so smart, I don't care what that crummy high school said. I was a lot smarter than Martha and I still am. Smart enough to know drugs are bad.

"Aunt Aileen?"

"What?" The commercial hasn't even started. It's just getting to the pause between the show and the commercial. The part where there is a short break in volume and the screen is still fading to black. I can't imagine what he has been waiting to ask all this time.

"Has it been an hour?"

"What? No. Why?" What could he possibly have

to do in an hour? He's three years old for crying out loud.

"Daddy."

"Oh yeah, right. Well he should be here any minute. But you know your daddy is not exactly a punctual man."

"A what? Punchal?"

"He's not always on time. Punctual"

"Can I see him?"

"Yes, you can see him. I am not going to make you go outside in the snow." This kid is a real ripe tomato these days.

"Mommy said I can't see him."

"I already told you Len Len that you just can't tell your mom. If you do you won't ever, ever, ever see your dad ever again. Got it?" This should do the trick. I can already see the anguish in his face to think of never seeing his father again.

"Okay."

"You sure?"

"Yes Aunt Aileen."

"Good, now hush. I think the show is coming back on." I know the show isn't actually coming on for at least one more commercial but I need a minute to prepare for the show.

"Okay."

As I am preparing for the show to start back up I wonder what will happen if Martha really does come back at three or four. Len could still be here. It takes him forever to leave. Of course that's only when I want him to go. Now when he wants to leave, he just up and goes. Sometimes with no warning or as much as a good bye. Not that it matters all that much. Martha will just take Len Len without a word and stare daggers at me as she leaves. She'll be over it by the next time she can't find anyone else in the whole wide world to watch her son and finds herself crawling over here. This worry is all for naught because Martha won't be back by three or four anyhow.

Just as my thoughts of Martha are winding down and my show is about to wind back up there is a knock at the door, followed by it swinging open.

"Daddy!" He gets this out of his little mouth before I am even turned around.

I realize now that it has been some time since Len Len must have seen his father. What a shame that poor unhappy Martha must punish her son to punish Lenny. All of this just because she can no longer have him.

"Hey there Lenny my boy," he sounds a bit over excited. "How goes it?" He sounds almost like he is still drunk from the night before. Not that kind of hung over drunk; the one where he drank so much the night before that when he wakes up there are still traces of drunk clinging to him from the previous evening. I would say that this drunk has shades of that previous kind of drunk in addition to a few morning pops.

"Lenny quiet down, don't make such a racket. My shows are on."

"Oh your shows are on. You are right, that is more important than me seeing my son for the first time in months." Unfortunately his sarcasm can't be missed. I am fortunate that it can, however, be ignored.

"Daddy can we go to the pawk?"

"The pawk? No. But if you're good we can go to the park when it gets warmer outside."

"I said the pawk."

"It's park with an 'R'. Don't say it like a queer."

"Why don't the two of you go to the pawk, or the park, or anywhere else and finish your conversation. I am trying to watch my shows." I am not sure if I am annoyed that they are talking or that my show is taking a turn that I don't care for. The only way I can figure it out is by eliminating one of the annoyances, and I'm not turning off my show.

"Well why don't I make a drink and then we'll join you for your shows."

"Fine, as long as you will be quiet. The both of

you."

"No ice daddy." He just can't let that go.

"That's no problem. I will start making the drink. I need you to go out and make four little snowballs. Pack them as tight as you can and then bring them in to me." I couldn't listen to my show and him at the same time. Rather than say anything and prolong the conversation longer I just sit back and listen to him while simultaneously wishing him quiet. I must admit the snowball idea is pretty resourceful.

"Make sure you don't use dirty snow. Use the whitest snow you can find." Lenny has to holler this because Len Len has already thrown on his shoes and is halfway out the door.

"He sure is excited to make some snow balls." I say this to Lenny forgetting that I was supposed to be watching my show.

"He's excited to make snow balls for me," he says proudly. "Aren't you supposed to be watching your all important show?"

"I am watching, so be quiet and make your drink."

"Okay. Do you want one?"

I shake my head side to side quickly so he knows that I am trying to watch my show and want no further interruptions.

Lenny finishes making his drink and plops down next to me on the couch. I try to ignore his almost popping the cushion with his cannonball landing. That is until he flops over to kiss my cheek and in the process spills some of his drink.

"Damn it Lenny. I haven't even finished paying off this couch yet and you're already ruining it."

"Settle down babe. I just wanted to start with a kiss."

"Well that's where it starts and ends for now. Len Len will be back any minute and Martha isn't too far off herself so you just settle down there big fella." I say this knowing that Martha probably won't be back anytime soon and that he won't settle down either.

"Are you kidding me? That boy is probably making a snowman by now. He won't be back for at least thirty minutes. Which gives us plenty of time to have ourselves a little fun babe." I am not sure if this is a request or a proposition.

"Here daddy," Len Len comes bounding over the couch to put four perfect little snowballs in his fathers drink.

"Great job, Lenny." As he says this I give Lenny an 'I told you so' look.

I notice that he is clutching several more junior snow balls in his other hand. "There will be no snow ball fights in this house so you can take those other ones back outside Len Len."

"They for my pop Aunt Aileen."

This makes me feel stupid so I don't say anything and turn my attention back to my shows.

"Daddy can I have a sip sip?"

"No Lenny this drink is for big boys."

"I am a big boy."

Lenny looks to me and I give him a shrug.

"Okay, but just one." Lenny doesn't know that he has already had a couple swigs from my glass. I hope that this next one is enough to get him to fall asleep before my good show comes on.

After Len Len takes another sip his face starts out in extreme disagreement but fades to a proud smile. He then jumps up into Lenny's lap. He sits there quietly for awhile. I don't know for how long but I do know that it spanned two separate commercial breaks. It is at the beginning of the third commercial break that Len moves him quickly and quietly to the love seat adjacent to us. It takes a moment for me to realize that he is asleep. He then goes to the kitchen and I hear him making another drink.

As he sits down next to me I can't help but notice that he has forgone the snowballs this time and is ingesting it warm. I also can't ignore how closely, and gently, he has sat next to me. I can feel what he has on his mind.

"Hey baby," he says this as he sets down his drink, "it sure is quiet all of a sudden."

"I think he is passed out from all the vodka."

"I only gave him two sips. But as long as he is passed out we should take advantage of it." He flashes a suggestive grin.

"I am going to take advantage of it and watch my show in peace and quiet. You are more than welcome to join me if you can be quiet and behave yourself." I hope that he can tell I am serious.

"Oh I'll behave myself," he says this as he puts his hand in my lap.

"I'm serious. I want to watch this show."

"Come on babe, I'm horny."

"Well maybe if you hadn't of passed out last night you wouldn't be." I give him a stern look as I say this.

"Oh come on babe, don't be like that. Just give me one kiss."

"No."

"Come on, your show is on a commercial. Just one kiss and I'll cut it out when the show comes back on. I promise." I know he is lying but maybe if I give him one kiss he will lay off when the show comes back on.

I let him in for a kiss. He immediately darts his

tongue into my mouth. I presume that this is still just kissing and I exchange my tongue with his. Then I feel his hand slip back into my lap. I try and back off but I don't want to entirely. This is when I feel his other hand reach around the back of my neck. He pulls me in tighter. I know he did this last move because the commercial is over and he doesn't want me to pull away, but at this point that isn't necessary. I am definitely into it. He removes his hand from my lap and starts to loosen his belt. I try to pull away but he just places more pressure on my neck. After a little more struggle I manage to slip out of his grasp.

"What are you doing?" I whisper.

"You'll see." He doesn't whisper.

"No way, not with Len Len right there. And keep it down; I don't want him to wake up."

"Oh come on, he's passed out. You said it yourself just a minute ago."

"Let's just wait until after Martha picks him up." I don't really want to wait that long, especially since I don't know how long that will even be.

"I can't wait that long baby. That could be days." I smile at this.

"Okay well let's go to my room," I say and then add, "Quietly." I start to get up but he grabs me.

"I don't want to go to your room. I like it right

59

here."

"Absolutly not!" I forget to whisper this time. Although I don't think it matters because he hasn't whispered since we started this whole conversation and Len Len hasn't moved.

"Come on baby. We can just stay here and be quiet."

"Listen Lenny I am going to get up and go to my room. You are more than welcome to join me."

With that I stand up and head for my room. I am pretty sure that he is going to follow me but you never can tell with such a stubborn man. I glance back as I get to my bedroom door. I notice that he hasn't moved an inch except to pick up his drink. I turn around and head into my room.

Once I am in the room and on the bed I realize that I have a problem. I am hot. I am burning up for him now that he has gotten me in the mood. He better get in here soon. I am watching the clock and as the minutes tick past I begin to realize that he has no intention of joining me.

Now I am beginning to think that maybe I should go back out there if he won't come in here. Maybe we can keep quiet. Not to mention that Len Len has had a few slugs of vodka and cola. At his age that should be enough to keep him passed out for quite awhile.

I know that I shouldn't. But why shouldn't I? He

isn't my son. I didn't leave him somewhere so I could go get high and blow all the rent and food money. These are the thoughts that are rummaging my head as I make my way back to the couch.

FOUR

August 24, 1982

"I don't want to."

"Do you hear that Trav? He doesn't want to." I say this over my shoulder so Travis can hear me.

"What if he catches me?"

"Mr. Nowak? You're scared of Mr. Nowak? That old Polack won't even think you're taking anything. He trusts everyone. Plus he is in love with your grandma." My mom told me that. I am not sure why anyone would love that mean old lady. She is always keeping our soccer balls and hockey pucks when they land on her lawn, unless we can hop the fence and get them before she notices.

"Can't we just go home? We're not supposed to be here."

"Listen Len if you don't want to do this than you can just go back home now. By yourself!" Just looking at his face I know that he is way too scared to go home all alone. "Now get in there and go get the candy and football cards."

"Why can't you go do it Joey?"

"Because we are too big." I say this pointing at Travis. "But we used to do this all the time when we were little like you. We are going into fifth grade after this summer. If we don't buy anything when we go in it will look suspicious."

"Look what?"

"Suspicious. We won't look right." I don't want to answer but I know he'll just keep asking until I tell him what the word means. He has been doing that all morning long.

"I don't want to."

"Oh come on. It will be easy. Just go in and tell him that your mom wants a pack of cigarettes. When he turns around to get a pack grab as much penny candy as you can and shove it in your front pockets. Then grab a couple packs of football cards and cram them in your back pockets. Piece of cake." I look to Travis for agreement.

Travis doesn't say a word but he nods and smiles. He's good at playing it cool.

"Then you guys will spend the rest of the day playing with me?"

I nod.

"You won't make me go home afterwards and be all alone?"

"Listen Len, if you go get the candy and cards we'll spend the rest of the day eating candy and trading football cards. Sound like a deal?"

"Okay. Watch me cross the street."

"I will. Now get going, we don't have all day long you know."

As I watch Len cross the street I decide that it isn't such a bad thing after all that I got stuck watching this little runt all day long. At least until our moms get home around five. All I have to do is spend another couple hours with him and then drop him off at his door. His mom even gave me the key so I can let him into his apartment.

"Hey Joey, why are we spending our day with this little creep?"

"Because my mom said she would give me a dollar to watch him until his mom gets home."

Travis just nods.

"Besides it isn't all bad. We are going to get some candy and cards out of it. Plus if that Pollock gives him his mom's cigarettes on credit we'll have a pack of smokes too." I'm not sure if that will happen but I have gotten cigarettes for my mom before when she sends me up. The first time I needed a note, but after that Nowak would just hand them over, as long as my mom was up to date with her payment.

"Well I don't want him telling on us, especially if he

gets caught."

"He won't get caught and if he won't get caught then he won't tell on us." Travis is a real dumb ass sometimes.

"What if he tells his mom that you took him out of the building and that I was with you?"

"Travis, he won't tell his mom anything if we pretend to be his friends and tell him not to." Idiot. "So when he gets out here maybe you could try talking to him."

"I'm not talking to him. He's only four years old. I don't want him thinking we're friends or anything."

"Okay Trav, then just give him a high five or something when he brings out the candy and cards."

"I'll only give him a high five if he has the smokes too. If not, I'm going to keep ignoring him. That's my plan."

"Fine Trav, fine." Sometimes I wonder if Travis and I would even be friends if we didn't live in the same building. We don't even go to school together because he uses his grandparent's address so he can go to a school across town.

Travis and I spend the next minute or two taking turns seeing who can spit farther into the street while watching Nowak's. I am waiting for Travis to spit into the street when I see the door open and Mr. Nowak come out and hold the door for Len. I look at Travis and he looks calm as usual.

That's when he asks, "You want to run?" So much for calm. As usual, it's just an act.

"No I can't. I have to bring him back to his apartment later or my mom will kill me." I give Travis a 'you better not go anywhere either' look, but I don't know if he is smart enough to decipher a look without the words to go with it.

"Boys," Mr. Nowak calls from across the street.

"Yes Mr. Nowak?" I look at Travis and he has either translated my earlier look or just didn't feel like running all by himself. I can't be sure which it is.

"Come over here, and watch for cars while you cross."

I look at Travis and he has an unsure look on his face as we start to cross the street. I can't blame him. He was the one who told me earlier that he didn't think that this little shit could pull it off. I guess I should have listened to him.

"Hello Mr. Nowak." I try and look innocent as I smile my broadest smile.

"Hello boys. Why didn't you cross the street with Leonard and come in?"

"I don't know." Clearly I am going to be speaking

for both Travis and myself.

"Well in the future I want you boys to cross the street with Leonard whenever you are with him. It isn't safe for a little boy to be tottering across the street all by himself. Got it?"

"Yes Mr. Nowak." I am surprised to be echoed by Travis on this one, even if it is just a mumble.

"Okay, well you boys behave yourselves today."

"We will." No echo this time.

"Oh and Joey, please give these cigarettes to Leonard's mother for me. Tell her that I apologize for having you deliver them, but I just don't feel comfortable handing cigarettes to a four year old."

"You got it Mr. Nowak." I can feel Travis grinning as I reach for the smokes. He is almost always good for one cigarette on him at any given time. His mother smokes so many packs that she can't keep track of each and every cigarette.

"Thanks and remember what I said about crossing the street." He hands me the cigarettes in my left hand followed by Len's hand in my right. I gather that he would like me to hold Len's hand as we cross the street.

We turn to cross the street and I can feel Len about to talk so I squeeze his hand tightly. He doesn't catch the drift and begins to blurt out, "I got…"

"Shut up," Travis quickly commands.

"Okay now don't grab for anything," I say as we finish crossing the street. "We will empty your pockets when we get back to the field."

The field is really just an empty lot near the apartment building. A couple of years ago, when I was in second grade, one of the houses was torn down. It was an old abandoned house. It had a brick chimney that was falling down and a piece landed on the sidewalk once and almost hit some old guy. We usually use it to play football games, but the houses on both sides of the lot are abandoned so there is usually no one around to bother us if we get into a fistfight or sneak a smoke in the field.

The field is only a few blocks away but it feels like it's a lot farther; especially when you have candy to be eaten and cigarettes to be smoked. I hope that he grabbed plenty of caramels. I didn't tell him which penny candy to grab for two reasons. The first being that I didn't want him taking his time and getting caught trying to get a certain kind of candy. The other reason is that Travis hates caramels and I didn't want him to find that out. I am hoping that he picked only caramels. Travis prefers those little red gummy fish. I don't mind them but I love the caramels. I guess there isn't a candy I don't like, except for black liquorish. I can't even imagine how that can be passed off as a candy. I have never seen a kid eat black liquorish, only adults. If adults are the only people that eat it, how is that even considered candy?

We are turning the corner now and I can see the field. I am still wondering about the candy. I am starting to get nervous that he only grabbed caramels and Travis will think that I told him to and we will get in a fight. I don't like fighting with Travis because he fights dirty. Last week he hit me with a rock. I tell you what though; I would rather have to deal with Travis than have those pockets be full of black liquorish.

By the time we reach the field I have decided that I am hoping for the red fish because we all like those. Besides, I am most excited about the football cards and Travis is pretty psyched for the cigarettes. The candy is more of a sidebar at this point.

"Okay Joey," Travis starts in as soon as we get to the field, "let me get those smokes."

"Hold your horses Trav." I knew he was going to try and get the cigarettes. He's going to try and keep them for himself. That's bullshit because this was entirely my plan. He didn't even want Len to come along with us today. I guess at first I didn't either but it has worked out great so far.

"Hold your own horses and give me the damn

smokes." He looks like he is already pretty worked up. He usually doesn't get so angry so fast. I know better than to mess with him when he gets this angry though; even if it did spring up rather quickly.

"Fine, fine, but I don't have a lighter."

"My mommy has a lighter." Len adds trying to be helpful.

"Shut up," Travis snaps at him. "I have matches."

I can see tears welling up in Len's eyes. "Give the kid a break Trav. He is the reason that we have the smokes anyway."

"I guess you are right." Travis says this as he strikes the match and lights his smoke.

"Let me get one of those smokes." I say this as he is already starting them towards his pocket. I knew this would happen.

"What kind of candy did you snatch?" Travis asks this while he hands me a cigarette.

"Taffy!"

I am thinking that taffy is okay as I lean in for Travis to place the lit end of his cigarette against the unlit end of mine. We can save a match this way.

"What kind?" Travis barks.

"Red." Red is not a flavor but I guess it is when you are only four years old. I am guessing that it is either strawberry or raspberry. I prefer strawberry but as long as it isn't banana I'm happy.

"As long as it isn't banana. I hate banana. It tastes like shit. Why would they even make anything banana flavored?" I suppose that Travis feels the same way about banana taffy as I do about black liquorish.

"Well let's have it already." I say trying to sound cool but not too mean. I don't know how much more Len can take from Travis before he starts to cry. If he cries Travis might head home and then I will have to spend the rest of the day with Len all by myself.

"Oh Shit!" Travis exclaims as he sees the yellow packaging.

"Len that shit is yellow not red, yellow as a fucking banana." I still get nervous when I say 'fuck' but I had to really sell being upset. I am pretty upset because I don't like banana much but I don't really care because I want the football cards.

"Kid doesn't even know his colors yet." Smoke pours from Travis' mouth as he laughs.

"Well let's see the football cards." I don't think we can avoid tears but I am smiling when I say this in the hope that we can.

Travis can have the cigarettes, Len can keep his crummy banana taffy, but I just want those cards. I am sure that I can get Travis to give me a couple more cigarettes and I will choke down a couple pieces of taffy, but I want those cards. I know Travis doesn't care about them and Len might want some but I am sure that I can just give him the shoddy ones. I will keep all the good players for myself.

"I couldn't get any." He says this as he sniffles. He is on the edge of tears.

"Damn it Len. What the hell good are you anyway?" I yell even though I know that this will start him crying. I can't help it because I am so pissed off. I am spending my whole day with this four-year-old kid and I don't even get anything good out of it.

"You're worthless." Travis doesn't seem to care that he is starting to cry either.

"No I am not! You are!"

"Good one kid."

"Okay, okay. Trav leave him alone. We have the smokes and the candy will keep him busy while we smoke them." I am still pissed but I don't want the kid to cry for the rest of the day either. I still have to watch him for at least a few more hours.

Travis looks at me like I am crazy. I try to interpret his look but it is too hard to concentrate because Len has blown out into full tears at this point.

"I'm telling my mommy on you." He says this

directly to Travis but I know that he means the both of us.

"No you are not." He says this as he pulls the cigarettes out of his pocket. I wonder what he is doing because he still has three or four drags left on the one he is smoking. Maybe he is trying to save on matches and plans on lighting the new one with the one still dangling from his lips.

"Yuh huh. I am."

"Nuh uh. You aren't. You are going to smoke this instead and be cool like us."

Len doesn't immediately say anything. He looks confused. I am silent myself. I am not sure how this is going to play out. However, I am not looking forward to it.

"All you need to do is breathe this in." He has already lit the new cigarette with his old one. He's clenching the new one between his teeth as he gives Len the instructions. He hands Len the one that only has a few puffs left in it.

"What's it taste like?" Len asks this as he takes it in between his thumb and pointer.

"It tastes good. Better than that banana taffy you snatched."

I have butterflies in my stomach as Len puts it in his mouth and sucks in. He immediately coughs it out and drops the cigarette. I can't tell if his eyes are watery from the earlier crying or the cigarette smoke. It is most likely some combination of both.

"Okay Len good job. You're cool like us now." I say this hoping that all of this will end and he will start eating his candy and shut up.

"Try it again," Travis orders. Amazingly, Len leans over and tries to pick up the cigarette butt then yelps in pain while jumping back.

"It bit me!" He yells as he starts to bawl.

"It didn't bite you dumb ass! Didn't you see me light it with a match? It's on fire. It burned you."

"Come on Trav leave him alone. He's already crying. Just give him another smoke and let him try again." I don't want him to give Len another cigarette but I am starting to get nervous that Len is going to tell his mom everything. Then his mom will tell my mom and I'll get my ass kicked. Plus I won't get the dollar my mom promised.

"Another smoke? After he wasted that one? You are out of your mind Joey. I am sick of this little twerp anyway, I'm gonna blow." He starts to turn around to leave.

"Wait, wait I don't want to be stuck alone with him all day. Just stick around and let's eat some of this candy and maybe throw rocks at the building." Travis loves throwing stuff at the building but we rarely do it because it attracts attention to us at the field and then someone might call the police. Then we might not be able to play here anymore, but at this point I'm desperate.

"I'll stay and throw rocks but not if that runt is going to be here." He says this as he points to Len, who is still crying.

"I'm not a runt!" As he says this he starts a rush toward Travis. His face is beat red and there are snots running from his nose. I am frozen as I watch him charging.

I want to intervene but there isn't enough time. Just like that, the whole thing is over with. Travis is laughing over him as he lay on the ground crying even harder. I somehow feel guilty, even though I didn't do anything.

"Damn it Trav why the hell did you do that?" I try not to seem too upset even though I am.

"You saw the nut. He was coming at me so I just reacted. Besides what do you care? He's just a little shit that we used to get some candy and smokes. Just send him home and let your mom keep her dollar. He knows how to get to the apartment from here anyway. You can see the damn building from here." He motions in the direction of the apartment building, which you can see but only because the leaves have started to fall a little early this year. You can't see the apartment building by the end of spring with all the trees in the way.

"I want to go home." Len muffles his wail just long

enough to say that and then cries some more, although he does seem to be winding down.

"See Joey, he wants to go home."

"He can't go home alone Trav."

"Well then you take him home, because I am heading over to the park to see who's over there. Maybe see if Katie is there. I think she digs me anyway. You want to come or not?" That jerk knows how much I like Katie. She can't like him. They don't even go to the same school. She goes to my school and we sit together on the bus.

"Lets take him home first then we can head to the park together."

"No way! I'm done hanging out with the psycho kid. I will just see you over there. Look for me; I'll be the one sharing a smoke with Katie." He gives me a wink as he spins around to leave.

At this moment I hate everyone. I hate Travis for leaving me all alone with Len and for heading to the park to see Katie. I hate myself for never asking out Katie while we sat together on the bus or while we sat on the bleachers during gym class. I hate my mom for making me watch stupid Len. And I hate Len for being a cry baby and ruining my day.

"Damn it Len! All you had to do was get some good candy and football cards. You can't do anything right.

You are never going to hang out with us again!" I am fishing for his key in my pocket as I say all this. "Just go past that tree and turn the key to your right when you get home. You can see the building from here."

I toss the key underhand to Len. As I turn around, and begin running to catch back up with Travis, I can hear Len starting to cry all over again.

FIVE

January 28, 1983

"Oh shit!" I can't help but belch this aloud. I am staring at the red tailgate of the truck in front of me and I can't possibly get much closer. By the looks of how mashed up it is I'm probably not the first one to see it so closely. I slam on the breaks and swerve out of the way with just a moment to spare. I use that moment to extend the middle finger of my right hand and wave it toward the driver of the mangled tailgate. I suppose that it wasn't his fault but he didn't have to give me such a shitty look as I drove by, so I guess that we're even.

I remember that I was trying to look at the clock to see how late I was to picking up Lenny. The damn clock was stuck on telling me the radio station. I can never figure out if I like leaving it on the clock setting or letting me know the radio station better. I go back and forth on this dilemma. I change the setting to the clock and realize that it is already a little after six. I am late to pick up Lenny.

I am not sure how late, though. Martha is such a nut case that I can barely listen when we talk. I think she said to pick him up at five. No wait, she said that she gets home from work at five and that I should pick him up when he gets home from school. Or did she say that I should get him from school? Maybe it was to get him off of the bus from school. Any which way I am late but I'll be there in just a minute so no use in worrying now; don't want to get in a wreck over it.

I see Lenny sitting on the stoop of his building holding his backpack when I pull up in front of the apartment building. I wonder to myself how long he has been sitting there. He jumps up and starts to run toward the truck as I put it in park and take out the key.

"Lenny my boy," I say hopping out of the truck, "how are you?"

"Okay."

"Just okay?"

"Where have you been?" He asks this not accusingly. In fact he seems genuinely concerned.

"Oh you would never believe me if I told you."

"Tell me. Please daddy, tell me."

"Okay but only if you stop calling me 'daddy' and just call me 'dad.' You don't want to sound like a baby. You're five now." I say his age so that he knows that I didn't forget his birthday even though it was a couple of days ago.

"Okay dad. Please tell me where you were." He is eager to hear a wonderful tale so I better come up with a good one.

"Well, while you were enjoying your day in preschool. Your dad was getting his truck back from a guy who stole it from him." Not exactly the truth.

I let a buddy of mine borrow the truck for the day so he could move his bed. His bitch of a girlfriend kicked him out so he had to get his bed and take it back to his mom's house until he can find another place. Too bad he forgot to bring it back when he said he would. So I had to get my neighbor to give me a lift over and grab the truck so I could get over here.

"He stole your truck? Why?" Damn, Lenny always has so many questions.

"Cuz he didn't have his own truck."

"Maybe he just wanted to play with it. At school I took Alex Finnegan's truck so I could play with it. He wouldn't let me use it. He was letting everyone else play with it. So I had to take it out of his bag when no one was looking to get my turn with it."

"Okay, okay Lenny enough about school. I gotta take a shit so let me have your key to the apartment."

"I don't have the key."

"What? Why the hell not?"

"Mom said I didn't need it today because you were going to pick me up right after school."

That bitch didn't give Lenny the key so I wouldn't be able to get in the house. Well it looks like that backfired on her. Instead of keeping me out of the house she kept her poor son out here on the stoop all by himself for the last couple hours. What a selfish bitch. I wonder where she is now. She should have been home by now anyway. She's probably out spending her mommy's money or giving her dad an uncomfortably long hug.

"Okay well then let's get outta here cuz I'm going to shit my pants if we don't get to a toilet, pronto."

We leap into my truck and head down the road. I am squeezing my cheeks together because I really have to take a dump. I even start to sweat a little bit. Wouldn't you know that this is when Lenny wants to start drilling me with stupid ass questions?

"Why didn't you come to my birthday party last week at grandmas, there were two kinds of cake?"

"Because grandma doesn't like me at her house anymore. Besides that's why I picked you up today. To take you out for your birthday."

That old bitch never liked me at her house. I don't think I was ever so relieved as when I walked out of that place for the last time. Like a weight had been lifted off these shoulders of mine.

"What are we going to do? Mom said we are going to have a sleep over at your apartment together."

"Well we are, but first we have to go out and celebrate your birthday. In fact, here we are at the first stop."

I pull in at a gas station so I can take a shit and buy Lenny a candy bar or a pop or something.

"This is a gas station?"

"It sure is buddy and you can get whatever you want."

We walk in and Lenny immediately darts into an isle and out of sight. I don't bother to follow him because I am looking for the attendant and I spot him near the coffee counter.

"Hey buddy, you have a bathroom key?"

"Are you going to buy anything?" He asks this like a real prick.

"Yeah pal. I just gotta shit first. My kids over there picking out all kinds of candy to buy so do you have a key or not." Fucking asshole.

"Here you go. Just had to make sure you weren't going to head in there and get high. I didn't even see your kid or I wouldn't have asked."

I take the key without a word and head to the bathroom around the back of the building.

It's just like any other shitty gas station bathroom. Dimly lit, smells nasty, cold, but it has a working toilet so I am pleased. It takes me a minute or so to build a nest around the toilet seat using the one ply tissue paper that they pawn off as real toilet paper. As I squat down I remember the end of the joint I still have left from smoking with Steve on the way to pick up my truck. I figure that this can only help to improve the time I spend in this cold, dark, shit hole.

I fish through my pockets, which is difficult to do when they are around your ankles, until I find my pack of smokes. I open the pack and tucked away in the bottom is the roach that's left. Only a drag or two at best but it's strong stuff and it will help pass the time in here, that's for sure.

In order: I take the first drag, shit, take final drag, wipe, and pull up my jeans. As I am heading out the door I wish I would have saved the last drag for after I pulled up my jeans. I'm not that broke up about it because that would have been tough since the joint was too small to hold in my lips so I would have had to try and pull up my pants with one hand. Still, it would have been a better way to exit the bathroom rather than having to hold my breath.

"Here's your key." I say this while flippantly tossing it on the counter hard enough to hear it bounce once and then slide off the counter to the floor. I know this has happened only by sound because my eyes are fixated on the cooler in the back. My throat is scratchy and dry. I am thinking about grabbing one of those sports drinks but then I recall that only the first few gulps taste good. After that they always seem to taste too watery. As I peruse the selections I settle on a pop, but what kind? Cola is always a good choice, but I have cola all the time. Let's try something different. I notice the ginger ale but that's no fun, all the fizz of pop but none of the taste. I decide to open the cooler and let my hand decide. My hand is heading for the lemon lime when all of a sudden out of the corner of my eye I spot the root beer. Yes, a root beer will quench this thirst appropriately. I grab a root beer and turn around to see Lenny staring intently at two candy bars.

"Looks like you can't choose," I say.

"I'm not sure which one I want."

"Well then I say get them both. Two is always better than one." I figure that I have an extra couple of bucks in my pocket anyway and it has been a few weeks since I have seen Lenny. Actually it's probably more like two months.

"Really? Thanks daddy. I mean dad."

"It is your birthday. Now let's pay so we can go and celebrate your fifth birthday; you old man."

"I'm not old. I'm only five."

"You're going to need a cane soon just to get around."

He smiles at me and we head to the register. Lenny puts the two candy bars on the counter.

"And one root beer." I say this as I crack it open and flood my parched mouth.

"Eighty nine cents." He says this without looking up. Probably because he is scared shitless of me and feels like a dick on account of the way he talked to me earlier. He can't even look me in the eyes.

I hand him a dollar and he gives me my two nickels and a penny. I pocket the two nickels and drop the penny on the counter. With that we're out the door and Lenny is already asking more questions.

"Where are we going now dad?" Lenny asks this as he slams the door shut. I mean really slams that sucker hard. It's like he uses all the strength he can possibly muster up to close the door.

"Damn it Lenny, don't slam the door so hard. You're going to bust it."

"Sorry dad." He says this glumly and I feel bad, since it is his birthday celebration and all.

"It's okay. I just forget how strong you are. I guess it shouldn't surprise me since you are the son of my own. Just try and be more careful on that old door." I do my best to use a tone that will erase my previous frustration towards him.

"We are really strong dad." He says this and then opens one of his candy bars and begins to eat it. As I watch I realize that a candy bar wouldn't be such a bad idea right about now. Too bad we have already left the gas station. Then I remember that Lenny bought two candy bars. Right after that thought comes to me the realization that I was the one who bought two candy bars. As long as I paid for them I don't see why I shouldn't have a little taste myself.

"Hey Lenny, why don't you let me taste your other candy bar just to make sure it isn't poisoned." Lenny loves this trick.

"Dad it isn't poisoned." He plays along.

"I don't know, I think I saw some evil scientist in there. He was right next to the candy bars. He might have done something to them. I think, just to be safe, you better let me have a nibble." The game continues.

"Okay but don't eat all of it. Take just a corner." He reaches for his pocket and pulls out the candy bar.

"Only a corner, just to be safe." I grab the candy bar from his hand and tear it open with my teeth as I drive down the road. As soon as it's open I take just a little nibble from the corner. It's delicious. It fills my mouth with saliva and I need to take a swig of root beer to really complete the moment.

"Okay dad, is it safe?" He reaches out his little hand, covered in chocolate from his first candy bar, to reclaim the rest of his second candy bar.

"Lenny you know that scientists aren't stupid. The poison is probably in the middle so I better take a bigger bite." Before there can be any objection I take a massive bite that cuts the candy bar in half. As I am chewing I realize that there is no way that I can swallow all this candy without another swallow of root beer. Unfortunately this is the same time that Lenny protests my poison test.

"Dad, you promised just a corner! Please give it back to me, I'm starving."

It's just then that I remember that his mom left him on the stoop after school and he probably hasn't eaten since lunch at school. I try to talk but my mouth is too full, which is probably a good thing because I have no idea what I would have said. I hand him the candy bar with my right hand and tip back the root beer with my left, which only leaves the knees for steering. I must say that I am a pretty accomplished knee navigator.

"It's safe to eat Lenny, but I think I ate the

poisonous part."

"Sure dad." Lenny says this using extreme sarcasm. He gets that from Martha. She sure is a sarcastic bitch. Now she is passing that awful trait on to our son. What a terrible mother.

"Watch that mouth boy."

"Okay," He says as he takes a bite of the candy bar. "Hey dad, where are we going?"

"We're almost there. Just one more minute my boy." It's true we are almost there, but I suspect that this won't stop him from asking more questions.

"Almost where?" As usual my suspicions are confirmed. He sure does like to ask questions. It doesn't matter how busy I am he just fires away one question after the next.

"It's a place with video games."

"What else? What else?"

"Well they have potato chips and pop." I can tell he is getting excited.

"Is that all?"

"No Lenny that isn't all. They have music and you get to be the one who picks the music." He loves when he gets to be in charge of the music. "In fact, why don't you turn on the radio and practice picking our music until we get there?"

"Okay, I will. Thanks daddy. I mean dad. Sorry."

"Don't be sorry, just stop doing it. Next time I'll have to remind you the hard way. Got it?"

"Yes dad."

"Good, now pick us a good tune to listen to. It better be a good one because we will be there soon and that leaves you only time for one song."

With that Lenny starts to scan through the FM stations. He usually spends more time flipping through stations than he does listening to the music. I think he just likes pushing the buttons. He loves jukeboxes. Last time I took him to O'Donnell's that's all he did. I gave that boy a whole handful of change. I told him he could play video games or grab a chair to stand on and play pool but all he wanted to do was play the juke box. He must have played with that thing for hours.

"Here we are!" Thank goodness because Lenny changing the stations over and over was already grating on my nerves.

"Where are we?"

"O'Donnell's." My reply is met by a face full of skepticism, so I elaborate. "They have video games, potato chips, pop, and that big radio that you get to play with and everyone else has to listen to. They also have all of our friends in there! It's going to be a blast."

"Can I play darts this time?"

"No Lenny. Damn it, you can't play darts."

Last time I let Lenny play darts one of those pointy flying basterds landed right in Timmy O'Donnell's leg. That old son of a bitch was dancing around and howling until we all pointed out that it was just a dart and couldn't hurt nearly as bad as he was making it out to. That didn't stop Timmy from kicking us out of there for the rest of the night and banning Lenny and me from playing darts at his bar.

"I don't want to go here again." I hate when he whines almost as much as when he calls me 'daddy.'

"Lenny you cut that whining out. I'm trying to take you out to celebrate your birthday so you better show some appreciation and shut your mouth."

"My birthday was last week. You missed it!"

"Well I'm making up for it now so let's go in there and have us a good time." If it weren't his birthday celebration I'd smack him one. As it is he's getting close.

"I thought we were going to your apartment for a sleep over."

"We are. We are going to go after this." I grab his hand and head towards the entrance. He resist a little so I firm my grasp and quicken my pace. Lenny follows me and I open the door. For the both of us.

SIX

June 16, 1984

"All right parents if I can have your attention please." Holy shit; there are a lot of parents here. I knew that this was going to be a pain in the ass but I don't think that the entire gravity of it hit me until just now. All these parents are going to be leaving their five, six, and seven year olds with me.

"If you could just send your children onto the field for a few minutes while we have a quick chat. Please don't forget to write their names on the masking tape that I have provided and then stick it onto their shirt." I am met with skeptical looks.

What the hell have I gotten myself into? I guess the answer to that is I haven't gotten myself into anything. My wife Maggie, that's who's to blame for this. She is a tremendous wife; she cooks, and cleans, and does a wonderful job raising our daughter but she has a habit of signing me up for things. I guess it's her way of telling me that I need to spend more time with Liz.

"If you are here talking to us then who will be watching all those children on the field? There must be twenty of them, at least."

"Great question, ma'am." Here we go. "Our discussion here will be brief but if you feel more comfortable keeping your child with you please feel free to do so. Everyone else please send your child or children onto the field." To my surprise each and every child was on the field in seconds.

"Thank you so much for your time and thank you for bringing your children on time. I am going to start by telling you a little bit about myself and what the season will be like." I have no trouble noticing that many eyes are focused behind me on the field. I might as well use this to my advantage by keeping this brief. "I am Brian Lynch, and please feel free to call me Brian. I am twenty-nine years old and played soccer for eleven years. My daughter Elizabeth is on the team but I will not be showing any nepotism. Each child will play as equally as possible in each game. This is the youngest level of soccer and my goal is to show them how to play soccer, not necessarily how to win. I do hope that we will win several games throughout the year; however it will not be our focus for this season."

I turn around and gesture to all the children on the

field with my hand before turning back to the parents, "As you can see there are many children out there. Our roster is currently at seventeen children and most of them are here today. If anyone is interested in being an assistant coach please stick around and watch practice. If you like what you see and would like to help out please speak with me after practice." I can see a few of the fathers in the group at least contemplating my offer but I don't truly expect any takers.

"Finally, please feel free to watch practice as often as you like but you are not obligated to stay. If you chose to leave, please, please be back on time. I remind you that practice is from five thirty until seven o'clock on Monday, Tuesday, and Thursday. I will hand out our game schedule at the end of practice today." I hope they grasp how important it is for them to pick up their children on time. The last thing I want is to be sitting in this park while it approaches darkness for three nights a week.

Several parents can already sense that this is the end of our discussion and they seem to break into three camps. The first camp, my favorite, is the group of parents already on the way to their cars to go grab some time away from their children. I would gladly give up the seventy-five dollar fee to be heading off to a coffee shop right now. The second camp, I anticipate a few problems from, but nothing to lose any sleep over, is the handful of parents heading to shady spots to watch practice. The third group isn't really a group at all. It is the one remaining mother that has me already wanting to pull out my hair. She is surly going to gain my attention before I head out to the field.

"Excuse me, Mr. Lynch?" Says the voice that I am sure is attached to the woman who asked who would be watching the children during our pre practice chat.

While wondering to myself why I even tried to head toward the field, I turn around. There is no surprise as I am met by the correct face that I assumed. I don't say a word; just give a nod as if to say 'go ahead.'

"Well my boy, Carl, is so small compared to the rest of the team. He just recently turned five and I am nervous that he might get hurt by one of the older boys on the team."

"Ma'am, you do not have anything to worry about. I am certified in CPR and first aide. I will do everything in my power to keep our practices safe and fun." I know better than to think that this is the end of our conversation.

"Yes I understand that coach, but how long have you been coaching, you seem so young." I expected at least one parent to be a pain in the ass but I wasn't prepared for her to be showing herself so early. I figured some soccer mom or dad would complain after the first game about junior not getting enough playing time.

"Well I appreciate the compliment but as I said I am nearly thirty years old and played soccer for over a decade. I think I am quite qualified to be coaching this team." Take that and shove it up your ass.

"I am sure that you are Mr. Lynch but you didn't exactly answer my question, now did you?" I am not sure if she thinks she is being diplomatic or if she knows that she is being a bitch.

"And what question was that ma'am." I try to suppress it but I do let out a sly smile. I don't want to create a war with this lady on the first day of a two-month season but I won't stop from doing just that if she keeps this shit up.

"How long you have been coaching young children in soccer?"

"Since you ask, this is actually my first year as a coach." I enjoy saying this knowing it will fluster her. In fact I repeat myself just to enjoy it again, "First year."

"Maybe you can find a more experienced coach to help you along this first season. You know, until you get your feet wet." I don't think that even she thinks she is being helpful at this point.

"I appreciate your suggestion and I hope that you can possibly speak with some of the other parents and see if one of our player's dad or uncle has any experience coaching. Otherwise I suppose I'll just have to learn on the fly." As I am finishing my sentence I see a van pulling into the parking lot. I am hopeful that this is the boy on my roster that has not shown up yet. It will give me a perfect out for this conversation.

"If that is the only choice that we have then that is what I suppose I will do." I am barely listening to the words but I am most definitely picking up the pain in the ass tone. I see a boy jump out of the van and figure it must be one of my players.

"Well I wish you luck. Now, if you will excuse me I have to welcome another player and meet his or her parents. It's been a pleasure talking to you." I waste no time in heading toward the driver side door of the van that has just opened.

On my walk over I recognize the face of the driver but cannot place how or from where that I know him. He doesn't seem to recognize me as I shake his hand and introduce myself. He tells me that his name is Walter Kingston. I know that I know that name. He introduces me to his grandson Leonard and I hand him the tape to write the boy's name on.

Leonard seems pretty excited to get on the field. He is bopping around while Walter tries to write his name on the tape. He made the mistake of putting the tape on first rather then writing it on the tape and then sticking it to the shirt. Leonard looks like he might be a little athlete. He is going to be smaller than most of the players on the team but that's partly because he is only six years old according to the roster.

"He sure does have a lot of energy," I say as he heads off to the field.

"Sorry that we were late. I didn't get out of work as early as I had planned." His grandfather says this with a very tired voice. He looks so familiar that it is killing me to try and place how I know him. "His mother Martha will be here to pick him up at seven today but on most days you will be seeing me or my wife." He is opening the door to his van as he says his wife's name but I can't hear him. I am about to ask him to repeat himself when I place his face.

"You are Aileen's father right?"

"Yes I am. Do we know each other?" His face seems a little less tired all of a sudden.

"Not entirely well but I did used to play soccer with Aileen for a couple of years, when we were eight or nine." I always liked Aileen. She was real pretty but she stopped showing up when we were in the fourth grade. We never went to school together so I never saw her again. It probably wouldn't have mattered because in the fourth grade is when the boys and girls split up into separate teams anyway.

"What did you say your name was again?"

"Brian. Brian Lynch." I say this knowing that there is little to no chance that he will actually remember me. "How is Aileen? Is that her son Leonard?"

I am not sure why I am so excited. I suppose it's because this conversation is infinitely better than the one I was having just previous to Mr. Kingston's arrival. Or maybe I am just excited to possibly be seeing someone I know from the old days.

"I can't place your name but I will be sure to tell Aileen that I saw you. She may remember you. Anyway, no, that isn't Aileen's son. He belongs to my other daughter Martha."

"I don't believe that I know her, but I look forward to meeting her later. Please remind her that practice ends at seven o'clock sharp."

"You got it Brian." He starts his van just prior to saying this and the roar of the engine forces me to read his lips rather than listen to his voice. Then just as suddenly he turns it off. He looks at the field and then looks back at me and says, "Brian I think I am going to stick around for half an hour or so and watch a bit."

"Sounds great, I hope that you like what you see." I feel like this conversation has run its course so I turn and head toward the field.

Before I am even on the field I see that pain in the ass making her rounds talking to all the parents that have stayed to watch the practice. I suppose I am rooting for her to find me an assistant because seventeen children is a lot to handle all alone for the next two months.

I don't have too long to think of attaining an assistant coach, even though it dawns on me that I am unsure of how I would even use an assistant, because I stumble over a pot hole.

Damn It! I don't know why the hell I am even back in South Buffalo. There are plenty of soccer leagues in Orchard Park, where, I might add, we now live. But no, we have to drive into South Buffalo and play on these shit fields and have our daughter playing with these shit kids because Maggie's mother doesn't want to drive all the way into Orchard Park to watch Liz play. Imagine that. Busting my ass to get through college and find a good job, working extra hours to make enough money to move my family to a beautiful suburb with beautiful parks, and here I am at Mulligan Park stumbling over fucking pot holes again like when I was six years old.

Once I shake off the stumble I reach the field and spend the next couple minutes just scanning the field. Seeing what kind of players I have on my team. I see the usual group of first and second year players. Many of them are just taking turns kicking the ball as hard as they can in any direction that suits them. Off to the side of the field some of them aren't even using the soccer ball, opting instead to play tag.

As I watch more intently I realize that they are not playing a game of tag after all. One of the boys is chasing some of the girls. I suppose that is what they do at this age, with cooties and all. Unless I am mistaken I believe that to be the boy that was just dropped off by Mr. Kingston. I turn and see Mr. Kingston watching the boy as well and I figure that I better go and say something to the boy. What the hell was his name? I believe it is Leonard but I am not sure so I decide instead to call the whole team over.

I sound my whistle and holler, "Bring it in gang, bring it in." I feel nervous as seventeen stampeding children head my way. To my relief they stop just short of trampling me and in unison look to me for instruction. I am not even sure what to say because I did not expect that to go so smoothly.

"Okay well we are here to learn the game of soccer," I sneak a look at the boys name tag and see that it is Leonard, "not to chase the girls. You got that Leonard?" I look right at Leonard and he is picking his nose.

"Ew, he is picking his nose," Shrieks one of the girls. Not just any one of the girls either. It is my own daughter

Liz.

"Elizabeth he wasn't picking his nose. He was scratching it." I don't want Leonard to be getting picked on so soon. I am hoping that all of his energy translates into a fine soccer player, but I must admit after getting a closer look at him he seems like a mess. He has stains and dirt all over his shirt, his shorts are way too long, not to mention that he has on old tattered sneakers rather than soccer spikes. While inspecting his sneakers I also become conscious that he has no shin guards on.

"Yeah Liz, so shut up!" Did I mention his mouth?

"Hey, hey, that is enough. On this team we don't pick on one another. Now cut that out and let's go over a couple of things. We are going to be wearing yellow jerseys this year so we need to come up with a name. Does anyone have a suggestion?"

"Sunshine," says one cute little blond girl named Julie.

"Oooh, I like that," adds the girl with the red ponytail next to her. I am pretty sure that her nametag says Meg but it could be Mag.

"Well I don't. I say we are the stinger bees!" This is said by a larger boy whose nametag says Mac. This is followed by loud agreement from the rest of the boys. I take a quick look at my roster during the cheering and realize that his name must actually be James McEvoy and that he goes by Mac, a typical unoriginal Irish nickname. He'll probably run into four more Macs before high school.

"Yeah, sunshine sucks!" Leonard again.

"Okay well we will vote on it at the beginning of next practice. As for now I think we should get some practice in. We only have about an hour left." It is more like fifty minutes but I don't think that at this age they can grasp the difference between fifty minutes and sixty minutes. "Everybody please line up on the line in the middle of the field."

As they all run off I call over Leonard and again remind him that we don't pick on anyone on the team. I also tell him not use the word 'sucks' or the phrase 'shut up.' He nods his head and I send him to catch up with the rest of the group, which he does remarkably quickly.

We spend the next twenty minutes kicking the ball one person at a time. I show them that they are to use the inside of their foot rather than the toe. The children enjoy watching to see how far each one of their teammates can kick the ball. I must say I am proud, but not surprised, when Liz sends the ball careening through the air the furthest.

Everyone cheers for Liz except for Leonard who is up next and seems to be growing impatient while waiting for his turn. His boot shows some promise. He runs up and swings that little left leg of his as hard as he can. His foot-eye coordination will need some work because he barely catches the top half of the ball with his foot. However, it still goes nearly as far as everyone else's kick, except for Liz's. It is encouraging to see that he is potentially a lefty; it's always nice to have one or two left footers on a team.

After the twenty minutes is up and each child has had at least a couple turns I send them for a water break. During the water break I look to find Mr. Kingston but he is no longer where my eyes last left him. I scan the small crowd of parents but do not see him. I look and see that his van is also gone, presumably with him behind the wheel of it. I want to tell him that his grandson was showing some promise and mention in passing his smart mouth. I guess it is for the best that he left. I wouldn't want to be getting Leonard in trouble on the first day. In fact when his mom arrives to pick him up I will only mention his potential as a soccer player to her.

After the water break we have roughly twenty-five minutes remaining for practice. I decide to ask if anyone wants to try being our goalie. One boy and one girl each raise their hand. I decide that this is perfect. They can each play goalie for one half of every game. Before I go and tell them this I better be sure that they aren't afraid of the ball.

I have the team line up at the top of the goalie box and have them take turns taking shots on goal.

I have the girl try in net first. She is a pudgy girl with glasses named Courtney. Courtney almost saunters to the net and then yells, "Give me your best stuff!" I must admit that she seems to fit the bill for a goalie. She is willing to and volunteering to stand in front of other people's shots.

Courtney did very well and I am confident that she will be playing goalie for us in the first half of most games. The only person to score on Courtney in both attempts was Leonard. Unfortunately he screams that 'girls stink' after each goal.

Next I have a tall boy with dark hair that matches his eyes named Justin take the net. He was our other volunteer and he sprints to the net and then turns around with his hands up in the ready position. Again, he looks the part of a goalie. I ponder the thought that we might be lucky enough to have two capable goalies. Unfortunately it turns out that much like my very first car, he looks better than he actually runs. He will be playing most of our second halves so we don't send Courtney in when we are already down four goals. In a comedic twist Leonard is one of the few people that doesn't score on Justin with at least one, of his two, attempts.

After the goalie drill I gather up the team and hand

each child a copy of our game schedule for the year. Before I even have a chance to explain the color system for games Leonard decides to speak his mind again.

"Mines all crummy! Somebody wrote all over it with yellow marker."

"Leonard that is called a highlighter." I direct that remark at him and then raise my voice for the rest of the team to hear, "I highlighted our games in yellow because that will be our team color. Remember to think about whether you want to be called the 'sunshine' or the 'stinger bees' and we will vote on a name before next practice so we can have our jerseys made in time for the first game."

I can see that many of the parents that had left have come back and are waiting to pick up their children. This pleases me because it is easily a twenty-minute drive back home for me and I haven't had anything to eat since lunch, when I took out a potential client at work today.

"Okay gang if your parents are here please go meet with them and I will see you here tomorrow." I pause long enough for those children to get up and leave. That leaves only a handful of children other than Liz still in front of me.

"Okay for those of you who are still waiting on their parents you can help me by picking up all the soccer balls and placing them in this bag. Keep one out of the bag and kick the ball to one another when you are done. Please remember that you are playing soccer so there is no using your hands."

While they are shagging the balls for me I walk around the perimeter of the field thanking the parents for being on time. Many of them take the time to thank me for being the coach.

I guess being back in South Buffalo isn't all bad, maybe I'll even take Liz to my favorite pizza place after practice. It's only around the corner from here and they load up on the pepperoni. I look at my watch and it is quarter after seven and the only players left are my own daughter and Leonard. I decide that as long as his mom is here in the next five minutes, or so, we will have time to grab a piece of pizza and still be home for bed time.

"Okay you two grab the bag of balls and come on over here." I figure the closer Leonard is to the parking lot the quicker he can get in his mom's car when she arrives.

"Hey coach, can I get another game paper?" Leonard asks out of breath because he and Liz have raced over here. He won.

"What happened to the schedule that I already gave you Leonard?" I am a little irritated because I am starting to grasp what a pain in the neck this kid is going to be for me.

"It had yellow scribbles on it so I threw it out." He

says this as he grinds his palm into his nose to wipe away some snot.

"Leonard I told you that those aren't scribbles. It was highlighter and I put it on there on purpose so you could tell which games were ours. I don't have anymore with me so I will bring one for you tomorrow."

"Thanks coach." He says this oddly enough with a proud connotation. As if he is proud to be a part of a team, proud to have a coach.

"You are welcome Leonard. I need for you to keep working hard for me. You have a strong leg and are mighty fast. But please remember that we are nice to our teammates and don't say mean things to them."

"You got it coach." That same pride was evident again.

"Leonard where is your mom?" It's twenty after seven already. It looks like pizza is out of the question. Maggie will kill me if I bring Liz home full of pizza and pop after bedtime.

"I don't know? Is she picking me up?"

I sigh and say, "That's what your grandpa said." I am frustrated that he doesn't know who is picking him up. I am frustrated that I am still here at seven twenty one. I am frustrated that I am here in South Buffalo. I am frustrated that I am not going to get pizza. Mostly I am frustrated because I am sure that this won't be the only time that I feel this way during our season together.

I am heading towards my car to find the folder with everyone's registration card in it when I hear a car pull in. I look in that direction just to see an old beat up pick up truck doing a U-turn and pulling back out.

I open the door to my car and find the folder shoved under the passenger seat. I flip through each card until I find Leonard's. It is written in sloppy handwriting but I am pretty sure that I can make out the address; it's an apartment building not too far from here. I shut the door and head back to Liz and Leonard.

"Dad I want to go home."

"So do I Liz, but we can't leave until everyone on the team has been picked up." I look at my watch and sigh aloud again; its seven twenty six.

"You can leave coach, I can wait here."

"No Leonard, actually I can't leave. I am not allowed to go until you are picked up. It is one of the rules of coaching." I am staring intently towards the parking lot. There is no activity.

"Well then I can just walk. I don't live too far and I walk a lot because my mom forgets to get me a lot. They let me walk home from school all the time." He doesn't sound so proud anymore.

"Dad I want to walk home from school tomorrow."
Here we go. Liz can't hear one thing that someone else does without wanting to do it herself.

"You can't because mom picks you up from school every day." I say this as matter-of-factly as I can with the vein hope that the conversation will end right here.

"I want to walk home from school!" This is not what I need right now.

"Well then ask your mother when we get home!" If we ever get there.

I look at my watch again and it is creeping way too close to seven thirty so I ask Leonard, "Do you have a key to your place?"

"What place?"

"The place that you live Leonard, do you have a key that lets you into the place that you live?" Damn it, I just want to go home!

"Yeah. Man, coach, you don't have to yell."

"Just go get in the back seat and I'll give you a ride home."

SEVEN

February 12, 1985

"This is not our church grandpa." I want to correct his tone of voice but instead I am going to cut him some slack on this morose day.

"I know that Leonard. I told you that we will be going to our church tomorrow."

"If it isn't church why am I wearing my Sunday clothes?" I am not sure if Leonard really doesn't remember the conversation that Martha and I had with him last night or if he is just hoping that all of this isn't real. Maybe he's too upset and in denial. I don't know the answer to any of these questions so I just remind him again.

"Leonard," I stop, kneel down, and put my hand on his shoulder, "this is called a wake. We are going to go in and you will be seeing all of the people that loved your daddy."

"Okay." He says this so simply that I am sure that he does not quite grasp the gravity of the event. He is about to walk ahead when I decide I better say something more.

"Now hold on there, Leonard." I tighten my hand on his shoulder slightly, "Your daddy's body is going to be here, too. He will look like he is sleeping. If you want to leave before I say we are leaving just tell me and we are out of here. Okay champ?"

"Okay grandpa." He says this and spins around. I have to hurry up off of one knee as quickly as this old body can just to corral his hand.

As we approach the towering double doors with the stained glass image of Christ I can feel Leonard's hand pull away. I am reluctant to let it go until I understand that he just wants to open the big doors.

I let go and he thrusts his body into the doors full force and they budge only a little. I tell him to try again as I arrive and aide him with a hand on the door and the other on his back. He glances up to give me a smile, I try to decipher if it is a proud of himself smile or a thankful to me smile but quickly give up deciphering as we are greeted by the staff of the funeral home. They hand us each a prayer card and ask us to sign the guest log.

"I want to sign." Leonard says this as I pick up the pen. I set down the pen and trade it for Leonard so he can scribble his name. For a boy in the first grade he still has dreadful penmanship. I suppose it is the boy in him because

Aileen and Martha had beautiful penmanship by the time they had left kindergarten.

As I set down Leonard I look over the guest log. I don't recognize many of the names and I am not surprised. I never met many of Leonard's family members. However, my eyes are drawn to the signature of my daughter Aileen. It is beautiful and unmistakable. I am pleased to see her name on the log and look forward to seeing her as it has been some time. It's too bad that we have to wait for Leonard to flip his car to see one another again.

After seeing Aileen's name I stop looking because I know that I won't see Martha's name. Martha and her mother are at odds and neither one wanted to be here with the other so they both stubbornly have declined to attend.

Things being as they are, that leaves only me as the remaining sole willing to bring Leonard. I emphasize willingly but not eagerly. No one had to twist my arm but I am in no way thrilled to be here. I suppose it is better that I do it than either of those two. My wife has despised Leonard Sr. since the day she laid eyes on him and Martha has always loved while hating Leonard Sr., often at the same time. However, while I do not like Leonard and in some ways hate him for what he has done to my family, I still can feel sorrow for another person; especially one who was so utterly lost.

"Grandpa let's move." Leonard says this while tugging at my arm and looking behind me. I realize that in my thought I have held up the line, which has grown surprisingly long. I nod my head and put down the pen.

"Remember sport if you want to leave at any time tell me and we are out of here. You got that?"

"Yes grandpa I got it." He squirms out of my grasp and walks toward the line to see the casket. The line is not terribly long but he seems restless as he leans back and forth to get an idea of how long the line actually is.

I join Leonard in line and as I am about to ask him if he recognizes anyone a larger woman who is crying appears as if on cue. Before I have any time to react she scoops up Leonard and, according to the bulge of his eyes, almost pops him. She lingers a little longer in the embrace and he nearly falls when she drops him to the ground.

"Don't you recognize your old grandma?" She asks Leonard as he clings to my leg.

"Now say hello to your grandma Lamply, Leonard." I say this confidently but I am not sure if she goes by the last name Lamply or not.

"Hello," he gives this sheepishly but never releases my leg.

"You don't even recognize me do you boy?" She asks this and seems to be actually awaiting a response. I decide that I better intervene because Leonard is digging into my leg pretty deep and I am fairly sure no verbal response is coming from him.

"Hello, it is nice to meet you. I am Leonard's grandfather Walter Kingston. I am tremendously sorry for your loss." I extend my hand, which she promptly ignores by looking toward the doors.

"So you are the man who has kept this boy from getting to know his family and his father better, are you?"

"Well I don't particularly see it that way Mrs. Lamply."

"Well I do!" She is quite boisterous for the setting and it is making me uncomfortable. I can't properly defend myself here at her son's wake.

"Well for that I am sorry and as I said earlier my condolences on your loss. It was a tragic accident."

"Yes, well, it was no accident." This statement throws me off and I am sure that she can read this in my face because she goes on. "That road should have been salted. Had it been and Leonard would have been home safe and sound instead of upside down and around that tree." She begins to tremble and weep violently as she finishes that statement. She is immediately met by two gentlemen who are being choked by their formal wear and they walk her out the door to get some fresh air.

As she is lead away all I can think of is how much I would love to tell her that I heard he'd been drinking all night at O'Donnell's place. According to what I have heard he was a puddle when he spilled out of there. I'd love to inform her that it's only because he didn't hurt anyone else or destroy any property that the police figured there would be no harm in not mentioning how drunk he was when he wrapped that junker of his around a tree.

I can feel myself getting angry so I place my hands in my coat pockets to hide the balls that they have become. I glance around the room and don't see anyone else that I know. While I am scanning for Aileen I feel the familiar tug on my arm. I look down and see Leonard pointing to a picture on the wall. No words just his eyes and finger pointing in the same direction.

I follow his gaze and finger to see the picture myself. Once my eyes are fixed on it I realize that it is not just one individual picture. It is a collage of pictures; pictures of Leonard Sr. to be more specific. There are many pictures of him appearing with people that I do not know. However there are two photos in which I recognize all participants. The first one is of Leonard Sr. and Leonard Jr. Leonard Jr. is only a baby with no expression. Leonard Sr. has a crooked smile on his face and seems to be quite inebriated. I am sure that the picture was taken in my very own basement because he is supporting his weight against our avocado washing machine. I am angered to see an obviously drunk Leonard Sr. holding his son in my very own basement.

I do not linger entirely too long on that anger because the second picture that I recognize is all the more troubling.

In this second, more troubling, picture I again recognize all parties in it. It is Leonard and my own daughter. He has her in a warm embrace. She seems thrilled to be drawn so close. He seems delighted to have her in such a secure position. There are only the two of them, Leonard Sr. and my daughter Aileen. I am trying to make sense of this picture when I am reminded by another tug on my arm that I am here to support Leonard.

"What's up kiddo?" I ask this doing my best to mask my confusion.

"Who are all of those people in the pictures with dad?"

"Well there is that one and it is of you and your father. Then there is that one and that is of your Aunt Aileen and your father. I do not know anyone else in those photos but I assume that they are all pictures of your father with the people that loved him. Do you know anyone in any of those pictures?" I know that he won't but I need to ask him something.

"Just Aunt Aileen." He says this and looks terribly sad.

"Remember kiddo if you want out of here all you have to do is say so and we will be in the truck and out and gone." I wink at the end of my offer. I wink a lot when I talk with Leonard. He seems to enjoy it and although he doesn't reciprocate this time he will occasionally wink back. I'll have to settle for an almost unnoticeable head nod.

"Aunt Aileen!" Leonard practically shouts across the room to her. On one hand I am slightly embarrassed but on the other hand I am also excited to see someone else we know. She gives a little wave and starts our way. I am not sure what to say to her as it has been a little longer than I would like between visits.

"Hello Len Len." Then she turns to me and says, "Long time no see," rather flatly.

"It's too bad that we are seeing each other here of all places. I must say that I am still pleased to be seeing you at all Aileen."

"Well you know where I live. You can see me anytime you like." This is said flatly as well but with an added dimension of frost.

"Well after what I saw there the last time I dropped in I would rather not." Between the stale smell and mounds of trash I can't imagine anyone wanting to stop by her place.

"Okay dad, just drop it. Today isn't about me for crying out loud. Poor Len is dead." As she says this tears well up in her eyes. I am perplexed at her emotion for Leonard Sr. I suppose it can be attributed to the fact that she is feeling such sorrow for little Leonard losing his father?

"Well it is nice of you to show up to support your nephew in his time of loss."

"Oh come off it dad." By this time Leonard and the line has moved on ahead of us and the line has wrapped around us like a garden hose around a tree stump. I know that I need to get back to Leonard but he is just a couple of feet ahead of us and I am confused as to what is going on here between Aileen and me.

"Come off what?" I am lost.

"I'm not here for Len Len."

"Well why are you here? Is it to see me? All you have to do is pick up the phone and I would be happy to meet you for lunch. I would love to spend more time with you."

"Oh how great. Thanks for offering to meet me somewhere dad. Heaven for bid I come over to your house. I wouldn't want to get you in trouble with that bitch wife of yours."

"Aileen, don't say such nasty things."

"Whatever. Besides I'm not here to see you either so don't go flattering yourself." She turns to walk away and I should let her because I need to be getting back to Leonard. He is only a dozen or less people away from the casket and I really don't think he should see his father like that all alone.

"Wait, Aileen." She stops and turns around but I don't know what I am going to say next and I am getting stressed because Leonard keeps getting closer and closer to his dead father and I feel torn between two places that are less than twenty feet apart. I proceed with our conversation anyway, it will be brief and I will be by Leonard's side momentarily. "Why are you here?"

"Don't be naïve dad." She is starting to get teary eyed again. I am at a loss.

"Aileen, please tell me what is going on. I hate to see you so upset." I can't stand when my little girls cry. It makes me feel the same way I did before a football game in high school. My stomach gets balled up like a fist, my mouth goes dry, and I have to pee. The difference is that when I was in high school I could go out on the field and get that first hit in and feel better. With my daughters there is no way to get that 'hit' in. I just keep feeling this way until the tears dry up.

"I lost Len dad! Can't you see anything? I lost Len."

"We all lost Leonard honey. We'll just have to pull together to help Leonard get through this." I hope that this will be the final exchange because Leonard is only two people away from seeing his father's lifeless body. Who knows what kind of shape it is in after being wrapped around a tree?

As I am turning to race back to Leonard Aileen says something that stops me dead in my tracks.

"I loved him daddy. I loved him and he loved me and now he is gone and I am lost and crushed and miserable and"

She is still talking but I can't hear a word she says. The image of that picture comes back to my head. The one in the collage; I look back at it. I am aware that Aileen is still talking, and sobbing, but I can't take notice of a word of it because I am studying that picture.

"Don't say another word," I command while cutting her off.

"But daddy I loved him."

"Well I suppose we all loved him on some level dear." I say this hoping that I have misread the situation completely, hoping that Aileen would never do this to her sister, hoping that I wouldn't have lost two of my daughters to the same bum. Any good will feelings that I had toward Leonard are forever gone. I panic thinking that Leonard has seen his father so I spin around and see that the two people in front of him are still in the same position. I use this as my escape, "I have to be with Leonard now. Please excuse me, we will talk later."

"We need to talk now dad." She is almost pleading.

"Whatever it is it can wait." I am desperate to get away from this conversation and her tears.

"It can't wait dad." I can't imagine what she will say next at this point but I don't care to stand around and hear it. So I turn around and see that Leonard is the very next person in line; just one elderly lady between him and the image of his dead father. I need to move quickly.

"I'm pregnant."

And with that one statement I am frozen solid. A million, billion, trillion, different thoughts are terrorizing my head. I can't be sure what to say next. I don't think that there is anything I can say. I think I need to sit down. Yes I need to sit down in my chair at home. I need to open a beer and sit in my chair. It is a big comfy chair and it is where I do my best thinking. I am stuck in a stupor thinking about my chair when I feel a tug on my arm; it is at first gentle but its intensity increases as I am pulled from the thoughts of my safe, safe chair.

"Dad, say something." Aileen.

"Grandpa, I want to leave." Leonard

I am not sure who spoke first but my eyes are drawn to Aileen first. Her eyes are puffy, there are tears on her cheek, and she looks as if she might fall over. I open my mouth to her but no words come forth. I look down and see Leonard still tugging vigorously on my arm. He is pale white, as if he has seen a ghost. I suppose that in some ways he has. My mouth is still open yet the words still hide in my throat.

"Daddy, please say something, anything." Pleading.

"Grandpa, I want to leave now." Whispering.

I am again drawn to Aileen first. I don't know what to say until I glance down at Leonard. He is whatever color comes on the spectrum after pale.

"We have to go." I finally manage to eke out this generally bland statement.

"No dad you can't leave me. You never help me; you just move forward anyway you can. Well, this isn't like the time I was smoking pot; you can't just kick me out of the house this time. I am pregnant and I need your help. Please help me daddy. Please don't go." She has taken my free hand into hers.

"Grandpa let's go. You promised we could leave. I want to leave now." He still has a tight grasp on my other arm.

My chair. I just want my damn chair.

"Please talk to me daddy."

"I want to go grandpa."

EIGHT

April 23, 1986

"Now Lenny, you go have fun with Anthony and you better listen to him." I wish she would have emphasized the word listen a little more. This kid don't listen to no one. I been watching this kid run all over her apartment doing whatever the hell he wants for a couple months now. He's gonna realize real quick that he won't be doing that once they get to my house.

"I don't think we'll have a problem with him listening to me Martha." I say this confidently because I am confident there won't be no problems.

"I'll see you both real soon," she says and gives Lenny a hug while blowing me a kiss.

"When?" Here we go with the questions. This kid has more questions than that guy with the mustache on that game show.

"As soon as I finish packing these last few boxes up."

I know better than to remind her in front of the kid, but she better not forget to stop by her guy and grab some stuff. Her guy is way better than my guy. Shit, that's why we got together in the first place. I couldn't take no more of those shitty undersized bags cut with laxatives and baby aspirin. I mean, I ain't no baby.

Plus she is a pretty good looking lady so I figured between her looks and her guy she is a pretty good catch. Not to mention that she's like ten years younger than me. Younger chicks ain't so great in bed but they sure do look better in bed. Plus, you can always teach a young chick how to be better. Older broads are pretty set in their ways.

"When?" I thought she already answered that one.

"Come on Lenny she already answered that one." She has a better guy than I do, she's young, and she ain't none to bad looking but dealing with this kid is a pain in the ass.

"How long?" This kid is persistent.

"Soon honey. Now run off with Anthony and I'll be over as soon as I can." She gives him another hug and blows me that same kiss.

"Come on kid, I got a surprise for you."

He looks my way and then hesitates. I hope this kid doesn't think he's going to be not listening to me too much longer. Pretty soon it's going to be my house and then it's my rules.

"Come on kid, grab that bag of yours and let's pop." This time he grabs his bag with the train on it and heads my way.

"Oh, and hey, Martha don't forget to…"

"I won't, I won't. Now get going you two." She already knows what I'm thinking. I like that.

We head out the door and leave it open so Martha won't have to fumble around with the door while she is carrying the last couple boxes. We get to the car and I tell Lenny to hop in the back.

"I don't want to sit in the back. I want to sit up front." This kid has the whiniest voice. I guess that's from spending all his time between his mom and his grandma. Those two broads sure can whine the second they don't like what they hear. I mean I only met the grandma one time and she was as over bearing and whiny as they come. This kid better figure out real quick I don't take none of that whining.

"Hey Lenny, I said sit in the back." He has the door open and is ready to hop in the front seat. I can't believe this kid. "Lenny if I say it again I will be throwing your ass as in the trunk. Got it kid? Now get in the back."

He slams the front seat forward and then dives in the back seat. He leans forward and slams the hell outta the door too.

"Hey kid this isn't you mom's grocery getter. It's a Camaro so take it easy on the seats and doors."

It is silent for the first few minutes of the ride and I decide I better say something. Martha feels that it's important that Lenny and I figure out some kind of relationship since we're all going to be living together now. I am not sure what to say but while I am thinking Lenny pipes up from the back seat.

"What's my surprise?"

"Say what now?"

"You said in the kitchen that you had a surprise for me. What is it?" The entitlement of this kid baffles me.

"Well if you keep slamming doors the surprise is going to be one of my shoes up your ass." I smile at him in the rearview when I say this so he knows its part joke. Although, it's part no joke too.

"Okay, okay I'll be careful with your doors." He doesn't even take a breath before diving back into, "So what's my surprise Anthony?"

"Well Lenny we are going to go to the pet shop. I figure with you moving out of the apartment building and away from all those other kids you might need a new friend." I know I ain't spending all my time playing with this kid.

"By the way Lenny don't call me Anthony no more."

"Okay, what should I call you?" He seems pretty excited. I don't think he is this excited to find out what he will call me; I think it's because of the pet thing.

"Call me dad."

"You're not my dad." What a dumb shit. I know I ain't his dad.

"Thanks Lenny, I didn't already know that. Anyway, your dad is dead and I ain't, so you can call me dad."

"I don't want to."

"Well that's too bad because if you're going to live with me then you're going to call me dad. You got that?"

He doesn't say a word. I look in my mirror and he is looking out the window. That son of a bitch is ignoring me.

"Hey Lenny I said you got that?"

He mumbles something. I have no clue what it was. I think it might have been smart assed but it could have been him saying yes. I'm gonna let it go for now. We'll just see what happens the next time he calls me a name. If its dad I know he got it. If it ain't dad then I'm going to have to teach him some manners.

"Okay we're here Lenny," I announce after a few

more silent turns.

I pull into the handicapped spot at Miller's pet shop after driving past some of the regular spots. I figure that there won't be no handicapped people buying pets anyway. I bet the city makes them put the handicapped spot here. I don't think no business man wants to waste his best spot on no handicapped person anyway. Hell, they will probably be excited to see someone getting use out of the best spot in the lot.

"I don't want a pet anymore Anthony." This little son of a bitch better stop calling me that. If it were up to me we'd just pull the hell out of here and I'd take him home and give him the back of my hand. Unfortunately for me Martha made me promise to buy him a pet to play with.

"Listen you little shit you call me Anthony one more fucking time I'm gonna teach you some fucking manners." I lean over my seat so I am closer to him and hold up the back of my hand so he gets the point. "Now get your ass out of the car and don't you dare slam my fucking door." That does the trick because he gets out of the car and shuts the door real nice like I asked.

We get to the door at the same time and he just stands there like an asshole. "Ain't you gonna get the door for me Lenny?"

He pushes on the door and it doesn't budge. He

looks at me and I give him a 'don't you dare give up' look so he plants his feet and pushes as hard as he can. Again the door doesn't move at all. He looks at me again and says, "They must be closed."

"They ain't closed Lenny. If you are pushing as hard as you can and it don't open what do you think you should try to do next?"

"Come back when they are open."

"Damn it Lenny I said they ain't closed for crying out loud. Now if they ain't closed, and the door don't open when you push on it, what else can you try to do so you can get into the building?"

"Knock?" This kid is a moron.

"Holy shit Lenny we ain't at somebody's house we're at a pet shop. We ain't going to knock so you better come up with a new idea and don't tell me to ring no damn door bell either. Now listen carefully Lenny; we are at this door and we ain't going to no other door, you are pushing as hard as you can and it won't open but the store is definitely open for business. You can't knock. So how the hell are we supposed to get in?"

He looks as confused as hell when all of a sudden his face lights up and he says, "I got it, I got it." Then he starts to walk away.

"Well where the hell are you going?"

"To find the back door."

"Get your ass back here. I said we ain't going to no other door. You need to open up your ears or I'll open them up for you. You got that? Now get over here and try pulling on the door Lenny."

He drags his feet as he walks and then pulls the door open. As he does some bells that are tied to the handle on the other side begin crashing into one another signaling to the owner that someone has come into his store.

"Hello there fellas, what can I help you with today?" This guy looks like he spends a little too much time with the animals. He has on this goofy ass T-shirt with a whole bunch of animals on it. Isn't it bad enough that he spends all his time with these animals but, no, he needs to wear a shirt picturing the same animals that he already spends his whole day with?

"I want a puppy?" Lenny chimes in from more than an arms length away. It's a damn good thing for him too because if he were any closer I'd crack him one for speaking out of turn.

"We ain't here for no damn puppy." I say this at Lenny then turn to the store guy and say, "Sorry sir for my boy speaking out of line. We are going to spend some time looking around first. We'll holler when we have made our decision on a pet."

"Okay, well my name is Chris and I'll be over there feeding the fish if you need anything." Chris turns and heads off toward all the brightly glowing tanks.

"Great. We might even see you over there." Fish are easy.

"I want a puppy."

"Listen up Lenny and listen good. You speak when spoken to. I don't want to catch you interrupting adults again."

"I want a puppy." It's like he doesn't even listen.

"Well we ain't getting one so shut up and think of something else."

"Why not?" This fucking kid and all his questions is driving me nuts.

"First of all, because they cost too much money. Second of all, because they shit all over the place. But most of all, because I said so. Now think of another animal or we are out of here."

"Can I get a kitten?"

"Damn it Lenny you really don't listen do you? If it shits and pisses all over my damn house you can't get it." Damn kid.

"Well what else is there?" I can't believe that this kid can't think of any other pets than a dog or a cat. I mean, I can tell that this kid is dumb but he can't be this dumb.

"Well Lenny there are fish, spiders, snakes," I think about continuing my list then decide against it. "Why don't you look around and see for yourself? You are in a pet store, you know."

He gives me a look. I don't know what kind of look it is. I don't spend too much time trying to figure it out because the look doesn't last long before he begins his solo tour of the pet shop.

While he is looking for a pet I head over to the reptile section to get a look at the snakes. I love snakes. I love the way that they slither around slowly just taking it easy. That is, of course, until they are hungry and then like lightening they spring forward and nab their prey. Or until they have been pissed off and then they leap, without legs I might add, quicker than their sufferer can react and sink their venomous fangs deep into their bitch.

I am drawn out of my snake fantasy by the sound of Lenny's voice from across the shop. By the time that I am fully snapped away from the snakes Lenny is already full throttle into whatever the hell he is talking about. I don't suppose talking is the right word, more like shouting.

"Hey Lenny, shut it. I'm on my way over." No manners on this kid.

"I want a bunny rabbit!" He exclaims yet again

from across the shop.

I give him a quick open hand on top of the head once I reach him; nothing to hurt the boy, just enough to get him to stop yelling. It works and he shuts up.

"Okay now what the hell were you saying? And you better use your inside voice kid."

"Nothing." He is sulking. I hate sulking.

"Okay then, I guess we can leave." I turn to head toward the door and just as I expected he pipes back up.

"I want a bunny rabbit."

"Bunny rabbits are for girls and gays."

"I want one." Have I mentioned that he is persistent?

"Are you a girl?

To this he shakes his head no.

"Well that's good to know. Are you a gay?"

Again his head shakes no.

"Well then I don't think we will be getting a bunny rabbit today then will we?" I decide that if I don't help him out he will get some fuzzy gay pet that will piss and shit all over my house. I better make a suggestion. "How about a snake or a lizard? Some kind of reptile? They have iguanas."

"I don't want a reptile or a snake. I want a bunny rabbit."

"First off snakes are reptiles. They ain't separate animals. Second of all are you sure you want a rabbit because we ain't going to return it in a week when you realize that you got yourself a gay pet?"

He smiles and shakes his head yes. I figure it's his pet so why shouldn't he be able to get a queer rabbit if that's what he wants. It's not like it will be running around the house, we'll keep it in a box or something.

I look toward the fish and don't see Chris. I start toward the counter because Chris has apparently finished feeding the fish and he is behind the register now. I don't tell Lenny 'yes' yet because I don't know how much a rabbit will cost.

"Hey Chris how much will it cost to pick up one of those rabbits back there?" I point back at the rabbits as if he doesn't know where they are; he probably pets them each for half an hour every morning. He undoubtedly spends his time walking around the place talking to and stroking all of the animals when no one is around, while wearing his animal shirt.

"Well the rabbit will cost you seven dollars."

"That sounds fair to me. Why don't you get us one?"

"Will do mister, do you have one in mind?"

"I want the one that has the black spots. He looks

like a little cow." Lenny goes jumping in out of turn again.

"Damn it Lenny, was he talking to you or was he talking to me?" He sits there in silence. "Well? You better answer me boy?"

"I don't know?"

"Well let's figure it out. Are you paying for the rabbit?"

"No."

"Well then I guess he wasn't talking to you then." I look up from Lenny and tell Chris, "We'll take the one that looks like a cow."

"Okay mister. Let me ask you, do you have a cage?"

"No." This is when it dawns on me that he can't live in a box and I don't have anything a rabbit needs. Shit!

"I think you will need a cage and some pet food. You are going to want a water bottle as well." Chris is turning out to be a real Jew; nickel and diming me to death.

"This is turning out to cost a fortune." I look at Lenny. He seems nervous like I might cancel the whole deal. "Lenny are you sure that this is the pet that you want? You don't want a fish or a snake or anything like that?"

"I want a bunny rabbit."

"Okay, I guess we'll be going with the cow rabbit and all his gear." I am looking at Lenny the whole time so I can see how happy he really is. I prod him, "What do you say to me for buying you a rabbit and all the shit that it takes to keep a rabbit in my house?"

"Thanks Anthony."

"What did you call me?" He looks down and doesn't say a word. I repeat myself, "I asked you what you called me." Again his eyes are glued to the floor. "Damn it Lenny I warned you about calling me Anthony. If you ain't gonna listen then I am going to have to make you listen.

With that I give him one good whack on the cheek. It's nothing too serious, just the back of my hand. Enough to remind him that he better start using his ears around me.

"I'm sorry mister but you can't be disciplining your boy in the store." Who the hell does this guy think he is?

"Aren't you supposed to be getting the boy a rabbit?"

"Yes sir and I am on my way to do that now, but I can't allow you to discipline the boy in the store." He seems nervous about speaking up but steadfast in his words.

"Okay Chris then why don't you go and grab the rabbit and all the shit it's going to need to survive and we'll be outside. We'll meet you back here in five minutes." I don't wait to hear his answer. All I hear are the bells on the door as I push it open with one hand and drag Lenny outside with the other.

NINE
December 31, 1987

"Damn it!" I say this out loud although I am alone. I guess I was alone. I am not sure how alone actually works because I am in my house by myself but there is a knocking at the door so I guess I am not truly alone. I suppose I could be considered alone. I guess if I left the door alone I would still be all by myself. Although in my line of work I can't. I can't leave that door alone.

Oh sure, some people will knock for a few minutes and leave. Some other people will simply sit down on my steps and wait for my opening of the door for them, and others will begin to pray for my inevitable return home. Not that I go out very often. Some people will wait several hours for one of these two things to occur.

Even further still, a handful of people will kick the door in, thinking that I am not home at all. They will try and make a grab of what they can before leaving quick quick. So no, I guess I am not alone. Someone else in this situation could be considered alone but I am not that person.

As I am approaching the side door there is another knock; this one sounding more urgent than before. I slow down until I come to a complete stop. If this were my front door I would be more concerned. I suppose I would wonder if my mother were ill or I would think that possibly a motorist has broken down outside my house and needs to ring a tow truck, if it were my front door. Hell, I might even go and grab my gun away from the side door in case there was some trouble at my front door, if it was my front door. That, however, isn't the case. It is my side door.

This is the door that all my clients come to. It is the door that keeps them from what they want and, in many cases, need. That's it, just a door. I mean it is a formidable door. After a few break-ins I put up a new door made of some kind of metallic composite. I put the deadbolt on there myself. I do all the work to my house on my own. I don't want anyone to get the lay of this house in their brains lest they come back at a later date with a mischievous agenda.

I am just about to move toward the door again when I hear a knock. I guess a knock is an understatement; this is more like a pound. The kind of pound one makes with a fist. Not the part of a fist that you would use to throw a punch. No, that would really hurt your hand on a door like this, although I have heard that front of fist noise on the door before. That is usually reserved for someone who is really hurting and has been ignored for a considerable time. This pound sounds like it is being made with the bottom portion of the fist and is being made because the person on the other side isn't sure if I have actually heard the previous knocks. It is much louder than the punching fist variety but not as desperate.

I like this game. It is simple, yet it is easily one of my favorites. I like to wait at least one minute after hearing a knock before answering the door. If I hear a knock before the strike of one minute I restart the clock. I keep the time in my head just to make it more fun.

Some of my customers have figured this game out. They knock and then wait as patiently as their demons will allow them for one minute to elapse before knocking on the door again.

Of course, there are the sorry bastards that don't get the game. They'll stand there forever just knocking every thirty or forty seconds until eventually they'll be sitting there just knocking nonstop until I myself can't take the game anymore. These customers receive a scolding.

I realize that I don't have time to be playing this game very much longer so I unlock the deadbolt and open the door.

"Hey Max," He says. He's hurting pretty bad. Not as bad as some of the real junkies but he also isn't one of the high school kids that are just looking to score a little extra something for New Years Eve.

"Make it quick Mark I told you I have shit to do tonight." I look at my watch; it's nearly seven o'clock.

"Yeah. Yeah, I know that's why I come over before seven like you said. You said not to come over after seven o'clock on New Years Eve so I am here before seven."

"Thanks for being so punctual. Now what is it that you want?" Another game I like to play. Mark comes by two or three times a week and always gets the same thing every time. He never changes his mind to ask for a sack of weed or a bottle of pills. Every time I see Mark he wants twenty dollars worth of coke. Every time.

"The usual man, some blow." He says this as he reaches into his pocket for his crisp twenty-dollar bill. He has on no account given me a crumpled twenty; two fives and a ten; or a few rolls of quarters. It's always an evenly folded twenty-dollar bill.

"Oh yeah, now I remember. How much do you want?" I love games. It's fun to make him say exactly what he wants. To state precisely what it is going to take to rid himself, temporarily, of his demons.

"Twenty." He is facing me but his eyes are somewhere off in the distance. I don't want to even think about where his mind is and I am hoping he doesn't share.

All too often these clients come through and won't shut up about what's going on in their shitty little worlds. The zaniest thing is that most of my costumers are junkies and tweekers so I know most of what they say is bullshit.

"Here you are man. Have a great holiday." I am in the process of shutting the door as I say this. In fact, he probably had to hear the word 'holiday' from the other side of the door. It's not like the guy is paying me to be polite. Even if he was I wouldn't be doling out any kindness on this evening.

There is still so much to do and only ten minutes or so to do it. I guess there isn't that much to do. I really only have a little to do. I already have everything set out except for a bucket of ice and an ice scoop. I suppose that isn't much at all.

I don't know why the hell I am having this party. I guess it's kind of a 'thank you' to all my high-end customers, the ones who are more recreational. I don't want any of those junkies dropping by. I don't want any of those dime bag pot heads stopping over either.

No, I only told the high-end designer drug guys to come by. Of course I also invited every semi-sane chick patron that I supply. I told them to bring a couple girlfriends too. I figure hot chicks hang out with hot chicks so what's the problem?

Anyway, I figure that this is more of a thank you for sticking with me through my move out to the suburbs. It's nice not having to deal with nosy neighbor's one door over always casting judgmental and inquisitive glances my way, lofting their set up questions in my direction. It's much easier to do my business with so much distance from one house to the next. As long as I keep my lawn mowed in the spring and summer, the leaves raked up in the fall, and the driveway shoveled after a snow dumping then I am undisturbed out here in suburbia. I know it's been awhile since I moved but late is always more appreciated than never.

As I am placing an ice cream scoop in the ice bucket I hear a knock on the front door. I know that this has to be a party patron because I specifically told them to use the front door on this one and only occasion.

I am heading towards the door when I remember my gun is out in the open next to the side door. I decide that I don't believe any of the invites would be stealing from me so I think it a powerful move to leave it out, besides I have another one in the safe along with all the products I have weighed and bagged for tonight's festivities.

"Happy New Year Max!" I am greeted ecstatically from none other than Jacob. I should have guessed that Jacob would be the first one here. He is one of these guys who purchases shit loads of powder to share with his ladies. The ladies that we both know he wouldn't have a shot at unless he had shit loads of powder on him at all times. No surprise that he is the first guy here and that he has brought an armful of beauties with him.

"Hey there Jacob, it's good to see your friends," I say omitting him from the goodwill. I do say this with a smile but we both know that the smirk does not imply that it was a joke.

"Can we come in?" Jacob is eager to be inside my place. He has tried to weasel his way inside ever since we began doing business together.

"They are more than welcome to come in but you are on a conditional basis. I'll let you know if you receive full evening privileges in thirty minutes or so."

"You are a riot Max. Hey girls say hello to Max."

"Hey Max." The girls say this almost in unison as they all file into the house.

"Hey Max where is the can?" He starts looking around immediately.

"Down that hall," I point, "it's the first door on your left." I am made uneasy at how quickly Jacob has left the room. I sooth myself with the reminder that he is a half wit, trust fund, bitch who isn't capable of fighting off one of his girls if it came down to it. Still I decide to take the bullets out of my gun and put them in my pocket until I get back to the safe to store them. I still like the idea of leaving the gun out so I place it back where it was before I unloaded it.

"Max you sure got some nice place here." Jacob exclaims as he comes back down the hallway all too quickly to have used the can.

"Glad you took the tour." I say this with a bit of an edge so he knows I am displeased. Although I am not too upset because I have my room locked and the only key is in the same pocket as the bullets. My room has anything that anyone would be thinking about taking. I know that wasn't what Jacob was looking for though because he came by earlier today and bought enough powder for all three of his lady friends to stay skinny for a month.

"Okay Max, what's the plan for tonight?"

"What do you mean?" It's a fucking party. Get loose and try to get laid. What else do you do at a party? Thank goodness there is another knock at the front door and I don't have to explain to Jacob how a fucking party works. He wanders over to the booze table and his ladies follow him like flies to shit as I head towards the door.

I can hear a bunch of chatter before I even open the door. I can tell immediately that it's a group of ladies. I straighten up and open the door. I see Vanessa accompanied by three friends standing almost in a straight line, each person in line being clothed less than the one in front; starting with Vanessa in tight jeans and a backless top and ending with a blond in a miniskirt and a midriff. They must be freezing standing on the porch in this cold December evening.

"Must be cold out there." I state the obvious forcing them to ask to be let in.

"Sure is Max." They all look a little uneasy about the situation, except for Vanessa. I wonder what she has told them about me.

"I heard it was going to snow around midnight, just in time for the ball to drop." This is not even true. I suppose that if it is true it is nothing more than a mere coincidence. I am just doing what I can to make conversation until they ask to come in.

"Well I hope we make it inside by then." Vanessa is a pistol and usually pushes back when I play my games. I find it rather strange that of all the people that I screw with Vanessa is one of the few, outside of my family members, that pushes back. I suppose it's because she's Italian, her pops is straight from Sicily. I guess that would make her

Sicilian. Whatever the hell she is, it makes her fiery.

"I wouldn't want it any other way." I am clamoring to find a way to regain control but it is evident that Vanessa is running court at this point.

"I'll take that as an invitation." She says as she steps forward.

"If you must," I say while simultaneously smirking and stepping aside to allow Vanessa and her friends, none of whom introduce themselves to me, into my place.

Once inside I think of something to say to regain some of my advantage, "Well the drinks are on the table if you and your nameless friends would like a drink."

"Max this is Jenny, Mandy, and Julie." She points at each as she names them. "Girls this is Max and it's his party." She looks at me and winks as she makes her friends aware that this is my party and I should be treated accordingly. Her friends throw a smattering of greetings my way and I simply nod my head in acknowledgment.

This goes on for the next thirty minutes or so, people knocking on the front door and being forced in round about ways to ask for entry. Some of the guys show up with girls and all of the girls show up with girls. None of the girls show up with guys, as instructed. I am pleased with the girl to guy ratio, it's somewhere around two to one. I am contemplating how many girls I might leave for the other guys when I hear another knock at the door. It must be someone going for that fashionably late routine.

I am surprised when I open the door and see a family looking back at me. Due to the shock I don't immediately recognize Martha.

"Hey Max." She says obviously nervous.

"Hey Martha," I pause to look at the rest of her crew and continue, "This really isn't a family friendly environment tonight." Not only is it not a family friendly environment on this night but I think it's safe to say that I have never lived in a place that was friendly to any family, including my own.

"Yeah sorry about that but Anthony has been trying to meet you for awhile now and he was desperate to come."

"Hey Max, I'm Anthony." He extends his hand as if I might accept it.

"Who's the kid?" I say this to Martha ignoring the aforementioned extended hand.

"He's mine. We couldn't find a sitter. His name is…"

Cutting her off I inform, "Well this isn't going to be a good place for him tonight."

"Come on Max. We're already here and Lenny won't be a problem to no one. He can be your bartender. He's great at making drinks. He makes them for me and

Anthony all the time and they always taste great." Anthony's hand has returned to his side and the boy's hands are in his pockets.

It doesn't look like she's letting up and the last thing I want is a big fight outside my house on New Years Eve with my biggest clients inside. I guess the last thing that I want is the cops to be sent over, which could happen if we have a big loud disagreement outside on New Years Eve.

Either way I am going to have to budge and let them in but as I am doing so I have a great feeling of excitement. I realize that I am going to get to play one of my all time favorite games. I don't get to play it very often because of how rare it is to have a couple, or for that matter any guy that I don't already know well, in my house.

I can't even wait a few minutes to play so as soon as they are in I prepare to start. I see that the boy is already heading over to the booze table to make drinks or whatever the hell his plan is. Anthony is just looking around taking all the beautiful people in. Martha is following after her boy to either to tell him to behave or to have him make her a drink. My guess is the latter. Not wanting them to get too far away or involved in a conversation I begin.

"Hey Martha come here." I love to tell other guys' girls what to do in front of them. I see him immediately looking in my direction.

"Okay." She says to me and then turns to the boy, "Lenny finish making mommy's drink and bring it over to me." Then she heads in my direction.

I lean in close to whisper in her ear. What is being said does not have to be whispered while in this company but I know that it will drive that Guido she's here with crazy. All I relay to her is that if she needs anything to let me know because it's in my room. To this she nods and heads on over to Anthony. They are exchanging words that seem to have a little emotion behind them. Exasperated he reaches into his pocket and hands her some money.

She returns to me with the money that her man has given her. At the same time she hands me the money the boy returns and hands Martha her drink.

I look across the room at Anthony and say "I don't need your money; it's going to be on the house." Then I hand the money to the boy and tell him it's a tip. Redirecting my eyes at Anthony I add, "We'll be back but it might take a little while so why don't you take the boy down to the basement and use the pool table, it's going to get a little racy up here anyway. You two can play on the pool table just don't scratch the felt."

His face is torn between trying to act unaffected by my statement and trying to control his fierce anger; one of the all time greatest faces to evoke in a person. I can see him searching my face for my intent with Martha.

Maybe I just want to give her a free taste and chat with a friend, maybe I still have to weigh it out and it could take awhile, or maybe I just want to keep the boy from seeing everything that will be going on in this perverse adult world? Maybe more? Maybe less?

While he is left in contemplation with the boy I take Martha's hand and head toward my room with the safe. As we are on our way my other hand is digging past the bullets to get out the key for the door that I will be unlocking briefly, only to be bolted up again after we're inside.

TEN

May 2, 1988

"Go get me more quarters Sean."

"Sorry kiddo I don't take orders." Though, I doubt that this reminder will stop him from giving them out like a miniature drill sergeant.

"Come on Sean please?" I am pretty sure that he still has a few quarters in his pocket. We have only been here thirty minutes and have already gone through four dollars.

"Sorry kiddo, I am running out of cash." He'll bleed me dry if I let him.

"Use some of the money that they pay you."

"Lenny I have told you every week for the last three months that no one pays me. I volunteer to spend my time with you each week. All the things that we do I pay for with my own money."

"Okay, whatever you say Sean." He fishes another quarter out of his pocket and puts it in the ski ball machine.

I am thinking about what to say when all of a sudden the seven wooden balls begin tumbling down the slot like a diminutive landslide. "Can we go bowling after this?"

"No way kiddo," I say with a chuckle. "Not after last time."

"Come on, why not?" He doesn't look at me when he asks this.

Instead he chucks a ball as hard as he can up the little ally. It bounces around and settles in the forty-point slot. He doesn't get excited even though aside from the fifty-point slot he can't do any better; rather he reaches down and hurls another toward the holes. I think he just enjoys throwing the ball at the openings as hard as he can. I have already had to remind him twice today that he can't throw the ball directly; he must roll it up toward the holes.

"You know why not." He loves for me to rehash the problems that he caused the previous week. He really enjoys the attention that he gets while breaking the rules but I am beginning to think that he enjoys hearing about himself even more.

I wish that I could give him more attention but I just don't have the time. As it is with all of my studies I am having trouble finding time once a week. I wish his family were more involved, and then maybe he wouldn't have to misbehave all the time to get some attention.

"Is it because they don't pay you enough?" He doesn't even take his eyes off of the game as he deadpans this.

"Lenny I tell you over and over, no one is paying me any money at all to hang out with you. I do it because I think you are a neat kid."

"Well then why won't you take me bowling anymore?" He stops just briefly to steal a look. He is reading my face to see if I am being genuine about my explanation on why I spend my time with him.

"I have already told you that you know the reason that we can't go bowling anymore." I stopped indulging him with the tales of his own misdeeds a few weeks ago.

"Is it because I was throwing the ball down the wrong isle?" Picks up the final ball.

"It's called a lane."

"Is it because I ran down the lane to kick down the bottles?" Rolls the ball toward the scoring holes, violently I might add.

"They're called pins."

"Is it because I poured my pop in the funny sneakers?" He's looking at me and doesn't even realize that the ball has gone into the fifty-point opening.

"They are called bowling shoes Lenny."

"Is it because that guy who walked us out told us to

never come back again?" Reaching into his pocket to grab what must be the next to final quarter according to my estimate.

"He was the owner of the alley."

"Can we go to a different bowling alley?" Pulling has hand from his pocket holding another quarter in it.

"Why don't we just enjoy our time here at the arcade, okay kiddo?" I give him a smile in an attempt to hide the fact that I am growing weak from his constant questioning.

"Okay Sean but we are going to need more quarters so you better go get some." He says this as a new avalanche of balls has come plummeting down.

"Oh, are we?" He knows what I am looking for.

"Please Sean? Can I please have more quarters? Please? Please? Please?" For each 'please' he threw one more ball and now they are all jumbled up and slowly filtering into the lowly ten-point hole.

"Well since you used the magic word, but settle down and throw one ball at a time. Stay out of trouble while I'm gone." He gives a quick head nod, which doesn't reassure me at all so I add, "I am only going to be ten feet away at the change machine so I'll still be watching you." Again nothing more than a head nod.

I turn to walk away and he adds, "Better hurry this

game is almost over."

"Listen up kiddo. I know that you have another quarter left so just play one more time and by the time that you are done I should be back with a few more quarters. That's it after that, I'm all tapped out. I'm serious; now behave while I'm gone."

I pull out my wallet and am having trouble finding a single. There is a five spot but there is no way I am getting five more dollars worth of quarters. I am pretty sure we could go outside and throw rocks at the wall and Lenny would have just as much fun as he is having here.

I am fishing through my wallet while wishing I was more organized, when I find my train ticket. It's right next to my college identification card. Once more I am struck by the realization that I am less than two weeks away from graduating. It scares the shit out of me. I am going to have to go back to Boston and find a job in the real world. No more beers for made up reasons on random Tuesday nights, no more trips to the Buffalo Zoo on Saturdays with Mora, no more all night ping pong sessions with the guys, and of course no more days with Lenny.

I guess I won't miss the commitment to Lenny as much as the others because it has been really difficult to find the time, especially with all my tests, papers, and now finals coming up. On the other hand I will miss being able to help him, even if it is only for an hour or so once a week.

He's a pain in the ass but deep down he's a good kid and I am pretty sure he likes me too. I realize what I am really scared of is that I don't know how to tell him that next week will be our last week together.

I finally fish out two singles. I feed the first one to the machine and it accepts it smoothly. The light clicks on and after a series of clanks and bonks four shiny quarters drop down from the machine into a metal coin collector with a clink, clink, clink, clink. I am looking forward to the next set of clanks when I realize how crinkled the next dollar is. I can hardly tell that it's supposed to be George Washington staring back at me.

As I am repeatedly forcing, and receiving back, the mangled dollar into the machine I find myself again thinking of graduation. I am simultaneously excited at the prospect of my life beginning a new chapter and saddened by the ending of what I perceive to be a positive chapter in Lenny's life. I will write to him and try to visit once in awhile but I know deep down that when I get on the train I won't be heading back to Buffalo anytime soon, or often for that matter. If Lenny writes letters as often as he does his schoolwork we'll be out of touch before I even step foot off of the train.

The dollar finally catches and deep in thought I

nearly miss out on the excitement of the clink, clink, clink, clink. It sounds weightier this time due to the fact that I haven't yet removed the previous quartet of quarters. I reach down and feel the cool metal on my hand as I remove the warm quarters from the machine. I don't know why they are warm and it is puzzling but not puzzling enough for me to spend anymore time analyzing the eight little round coins. I slip them in my back pocket and turn to head back to Lenny.

As I turn I see a large man sporting an angry face heading my way, Lenny in hand. I guess he isn't really in hand. This hairy fellow has Lenny by the back of his neck and is not treating him as gingerly as one might expect a grown man to treat a child. I suppose Lenny isn't your average child but that still doesn't excuse this fellow's behavior.

"Is he yours?" He demands of me as though I have done something wrong.

"He is today pal." I say this as I grab Lenny's shirt and pull him towards me. The man resists for a moment and then lets him go.

He is big but not tall, definitely not as tall as me. I would say I have two inches on him. He is meatier than I am but what he gains in girth I'm sure I make up for with youth. This guy has to be approaching fifty.

"Well he was running up the game and dropping the balls in the big point slot." He seems far too angry for this to be the only injustice bothering him. I figure that it's probably because he has to run his arcade seven days a week to pay the bills or even worse, he is nothing more than a lowly employee at said arcade.

"Isn't that how the game is played?" I don't know if he has caught on yet that he pissed me off by grabbing Lenny like he did but the smart ass smirk and the wink that I give him should get the point across that I know exactly how to play ski ball and I am now engaging in a game of my own.

"Listen Pal just take this kid and get the fuck out of here."

"Excuse me?"

"You heard me. You two kids scram."

"Oh I get it. You think because you are older than me you can push me around. Well guess what big foot; I want to talk to your manager." This startles him. "Yeah, I'd like to let him know that you think cursing in front of kids is the best way to treat the customer." I'm picking up speed now. "I want to tell him that we won't be coming back here anymore to spend our money and I would like to make sure he knows that you and your rough language, not to mention questionable treatment of children, is why we won't be back."

"Oh yeah shit head, I am the manager," before I can ask he adds, "and the owner."

"That's a shame for you."

"Oh is it?"

"Yeah it is because instead of talking to your boss I'll be talking to the police about this physical assault and verbal harassment of a minor. What did you say your name was again, or should I just keep calling you big foot?"

His face and demeanor change as he reads my face to see if I am bluffing or not. I hope I am concealing the fact that there is no way I am tying up the rest of my day, and potential future days, with the police.

"Okay listen guy; just tell the kid that he can't climb on any of the games."

"I don't think so guy. You can tell him yourself, he is right here with us so stop ignoring him." I have got him now. I could probably get a free game out of him if I felt like it.

"Kid, have a good time while you're here just please stay off of the machines. Okay?"

"Lenny what do you say to the man?"

"Thank you." He looks at me while he says it.

"How about you tell him that you're sorry that you crawled up his game and then you can tell him that you won't do it again." I look at him while I say this and add, "And look at him while you say it."

Lenny does as I tell him, knowing that if I weren't here he would be toast, and the man walks away.

"Did you get more quarters?" Maybe he doesn't realize that he would have been toast, or maybe he does and he doesn't care. Either way he didn't forget about those quarters and he wants them now.

"Yes," I say pulling them out to show him eight, shiny, circular quarters.

"Woo hoo Sean! Let me get them." He sticks out his hand, palm up.

"I don't think so kiddo," I say while putting them back in the same back pocket from which they had come.

"Why not?" Questions, questions, questions. Questions that he already knows the answers to.

"You know why."

"Is it because I was playing the game wrong?"

"Bingo."

"This is bullshit."

"Lenny what did I tell you about that kind of language?" I don't bother to wait for the answer that I know isn't coming. "I don't care if you use that language with your friends, I don't care if you even use it with your folks, but I don't want you using it around me. Got that kiddo?" I add a smile so he knows I am not upset. How can I be upset when he is conditioned to speak like that and I am the only one who calls him on it? We only get an hour or two together each week.

"Okay." He is looking at the ground. I think he may be holding back tears so I decide to throw him a bone.

"Let's get out of here anyway. I happen to have an extra two dollars in my back pocket so let's go grab a couple pieces of pie before I take you home." Everybody loves pie.

"Really!"

"Would I lie about pie?"

"Nobody should ever lie about pie." He smiles from ear to ear when he is assured that I am not pulling his leg.

As we are heading out the door Lenny stops. I am figuring that he must have left something in the arcade and that we have to go back in to get it. He leaves things places pretty often. At least he remembered quickly this time. The last time that he forgot something he didn't remember it until we were almost all the way back to his place and we had to go back across town to the pizzeria to get it. If it were anything other than his book bag I probably would have left it and taught him a lesson on responsibility. Eventually I probably would have went back and got it for him when I had the free time.

"What's up kiddo? Did you forget something?"

"Sean?" He didn't forget anything. Something's on his mind, now I can tell.

"Yeah?"

"You really don't get paid to hang out with me?" Poor kid still can't believe anyone would want to hang out with him.

"Not a penny."

"Okay, then you must be my best friend." He produces a smile that is new to me. It isn't mischievous, or smart assed, or trying to get away with something.

"That sounds good to me kiddo." I send him back an equally pleased smile.

"Sean?" While I am enjoying this breakthrough I am also eager to get to the car because for a May afternoon it is startlingly biting out. This Buffalo weather is tricky, just two days ago it was mid sixties and sunny and now it is overcast and can't be higher than forty outside.

"Yeah kiddo?"

"Am I your best friend?"

"You sure are. Now let's jump in the car so I can get my best friend some pie."

I am surprised that Lenny isn't cold. He is not dressed for the conditions. He has on a bright orange T-shirt. I suppose when it's clean it is bright orange. Today it's actually dull orange, especially around the collar. His jeans have as many holes as a golf course.

"Okay, but I have another question."

"Can you ask it in the car?" I try to migrate us toward the car but Lenny stands firm.

"Will you take me to the father and son baseball game at school next month?"

"Oh kiddo," This is it, I better let him know, "I'm sorry but I can't next month."

"Why can't you Sean?"

"Get in the car and I'll tell you over pie." I can't bring myself to tell him now.

"No. Why won't you take me, I thought we were best friends?" He is getting upset and I can feel all the progress that we have made over the past couple of months rapidly slipping away.

"Well kiddo, do you remember when I told you that I was graduating in a couple of weeks?" He nods his head in recognition. "When I graduate I need to move back home to Boston."

"You're leaving?" He screams this forcefully while pointing his face right at me and thrusting his fists toward the ground.

"Not for another week. We can still"

He doesn't stick around to hear the rest. I am afraid he is going to run away and I'll be spending the next few minutes chasing him and forcing him into the car but that isn't the case. He heads straight for the car and gets in the back seat after slamming the door to the front passenger side.

"Take me home," is all he says when I get in the car.

"Pie first?"

"Home!" His volume is turned all the way up.

"Okay kiddo but I want you to think about what you want to do next week. It is my last week here in Buffalo so we can do anything you want." I haven't started the car yet.

"I don't want to do anything with you." The anger is still ever present but the volume is much lower. In some ways it is more frightening to witness how well he can bottle his anger.

"Oh come on kiddo. We can do anything; we can even go bowling again. I'll find a new alley that hasn't kicked us out yet." I still haven't started the car hoping for some margin of concession.

I am met by complete silence. I turn to start the car but stop. I think of something that may cheer him up. I turn and start, "How about this…" but I am cut off almost immediately by a seething yet moderately volumed:

"Fuck you Sean."

I turn front and start the car.

ELEVEN

October 6, 1989

"I'm hungry." Leonard spouts, interrupting us from our thoughts.

"Well we're trying to figure out just what to do with you so pipe down." I snap back rather impolitely.

"Mitchell, mind your manners. It is not Leonard's fault that his mother is late in picking him up." Amy tends to be more level headed than myself.

"I'm really, really hungry guys."

"So are we, and call us Mr. and Mrs. Shea." I know Amy is going to give me a look and I am prepared for it. I no longer have the ability to stay calm. Especially after all that this boy has put me through today.

"Leonard we are trying to figure out what to do with you. You see the party has been over for several hours and your mother has not come to pick you up yet. We have called your house a number of times but no one answers the phone. Do you have any ideas?" Amy says all of this while giving me a 'cool it' look.

"Well Mr. and Mrs. Shea I think much better on a full stomach." What a wise ass.

"Well I do believe that there are a couple slices of pizza left in the refrigerator. Let's go get a triangle and come up with a plan. How does that sound Leonard?" Amy says this to Leonard.

"That sounds great!" Leonard says this to me.

"I'll be upstairs." I say this to no one.

On the way up the stairs I am thinking that next year we are having a family only birthday party for Leslie. No more of this inviting your friends from school bullshit. There is cake mashed into the rug, pizza on the wall, and a tear in the screen door and that's just the shit that Leonard is responsible for. The rest of those children were at least attempting to behave but something happens to kids when you get them all in a room and give them cake. Between Leonard and the rest of the mob I have a splitting headache.

I am on my way to the bathroom cabinet to grab some aspirin when I hear Leslie making noise in her room. I figure that she must be playing with some of her new birthday toys. I know it's not the one that Leonard brought because I already chucked that. He brought a disgusting toy pick up truck that was missing a wheel and had paint chipping off of it. The best part is that he wrapped it in the Sunday comics, apparently with an entire roll of masking tape. I couldn't help but snicker, which got me a frigid glower from Amy.

After downing a small handful of aspirin I head back to Leslie's room. She is on the floor having a tea party with some of her dolls. I don't know which ones are new and which ones are old but there sure are a lot of dolls for tea sipping.

She notices me and says, "I am introducing the new girls to the group."

I can tell she is waiting for a response so I say, "I am sure that they will all be lovely friends Leslie." She picks up the teapot and starts to pour each doll a spot of tea when I can't help but adding, "speaking of friends, why don't you come back downstairs and keep your friend Leonard some company?"

Her look is unquestionably full of disgust. "That boy is not my friend."

"Well then why did you even invite him?"

"Because dad," she says with repulsion, "mom made me give invitations to everyone from the class."

"Everyone?" Why the hell would she do that?

"Yes," she retorts rather angrily. I suppose I would be angry too if my mother forced me to invite that nutcase to my birthday party.

"Okay, okay. Well would you mind coming downstairs with me until he leaves?"

"Sorry dad but it is almost bed time. After tea I need to tuck in the girls and say my prayers." I am about to pull rank and order her downstairs when I hear Amy call my name. I am hoping that she has gotten a hold of Leonard's mother, so I about face and head down the stairs, bounding down two at a time.

"What's up Amy my love?" I say this with a big hopeful grin.

"Ewww love, gross," moans Leonard.

"Leonard and I were just wondering where you were," Amy says as I am doing my best to intimidate Leonard with my eyes. "I told him that you were probably coming up with a Cracker Jack plan."

"I think you were just hiding from us," adds the miniature prick.

"I was just checking on Leslie. She was playing with her new toys." For this next part I zero in on Leonard, "She loves most of them, especially the new dolls." I lay some emphasis on the word new. I am enjoying my ability to be clever when I realize that Amy is burning at me.

"Okay hot shot, any plans?" I mean really burning.

"Well let's think about this." I am looking down

pretending to be deep in thought so I don't have to see Amy's look right now, although I am sure I will have to deal with her whenever we are finally rid of our final party guest. "Leonard you go to the same school as Amy so you can't live terribly far from here. Do you know where you live?"

"I don't know the address but I know how to get there."

"You're in the fifth grade and you don't know you're own address?" What the hell is going on with this kid? Is he screwing with me or does he honestly not know where he lives?

"That's not being helpful Mitchell." I think that Amy thinks that she is being helpful by letting me know that I am not being helpful. If that's the case then I don't think that she is being very helpful.

"I'm not being helpful? This kid doesn't even know where he lives."

"I know where I live. It's just a few blocks from here, actually." I am amazed at the intensity in his voice when he says this. I'm almost a little frightened of him. To be so young, and small for that matter, but to be so forceful is a little nerve wracking to me.

"Okay boys I'll take it from here. Leonard you finish your pizza. Mitchell you pour Leonard a glass of pop. I'll go get the envelopes."

I head towards the refrigerator merely from being conditioned to listen to my wife for the last sixteen years. I battled it for the first couple of years. I would ask her if she could ask me things rather than order me around. She always apologized and assured me that she wouldn't do it again or at least would try not to do it again. In the beginning of our marriage we would have this discussion every few weeks, then every few months. After the first couple of years we would have that same discussion several months apart from each other. I believe the last time that we had that discussion was at some point in 1978.

I realize while pouring Leonard a glass of pop that I have no idea what envelopes Amy is talking about. Rather than show my ignorance in the matter I just hand Leonard his glass of pop and sit down at the table across from him and wait for Amy to come back and reveal what envelopes she was referring to and, more importantly, show me how they will help our current situation.

"This pop is flat," garbles Leonard through a full mouth, which makes it sound like he has called the pop 'fat'. I know that he has said 'flat' because I remember that the bottle made no 'pfssst' sound when I opened it. I remember why it went flat too.

"Leonard the pop is flat because of you," I say in a measured and controlled voice so Amy won't hear me.

"You shook up the pop and opened it up right above Leslie, my daughter's, head. It went all over her and her friends. It also worked its way under the refrigerator so I get to spend tomorrow, my Saturday and only day off, moving the fridge so we can clean up the pop that you spilled." Spill isn't the right word because it wasn't an accident but I can't think of a better word without using words that will piss Amy off.

"What about Sunday?" What the hell is he talking about?

"What the hell are you talking about?"

"Mitchell, mind your language." From the living room? I don't even know how the hell she can hear me from there?

I am about to say more to Leonard but when I turn my head from the sound of Amy's voice to Leonard's face I am greeted with a big pizza filled, open mouthed, pain in the ass smile.

"Why don't you have Sunday off? It's part of the weekend." He finishes this question and statement while also finishing his slice of pizza. I fight the urge to tell him to close his mouth while he is chewing and lose the fight.

"Shut your mouth when you chew your food, it's disgusting."

"You're disgusting!"

"Excuse me?" I stand up and begin to circle the

table toward our little houseguest from hell. I am not quite sure what I am going to do when I get to his side of the table but it's not going to be a handshake.

As I am one step away I decide that I am going to pour his pop, what's left of it, on his head. Let's see how he likes it.

I am reaching for his glass as Amy walks in so I abort the plan and ask Leonard, "Would you like some more pop?"

"No more pop for either of you boys. It's nearly nine o'clock and I am sure that it will be bed time for Leonard whenever he gets home," Amy says as she starts to dig through a shoebox. Or at least what used to be a shoebox, now it is a colorful box decorated in many different colors with pictures of balloons, party hats, and cup cakes.

"What do you have there?" I ask while admiring the beautiful box. I am wondering who did it because it is clearly homemade. I am sure that Amy will claim that Leslie did it while in reality it's a safe bet that Leslie was playing with a doll or some other trinket while Amy did all the work. She is quite the perfectionist.

"It's the return address box." She says this like I should have some clue as to what the hell that is.

"Oh." I don't have any clue as to what that is.

"It's the box that I had all of the 'thank you' envelopes in." She looks at me and can tell that I am still utterly lost as to why this is necessary. "Each parent wrote their family's name and address on the front of an envelope so that we can send them 'thank you' notes after the party."

"That's a great idea!" She really does think of everything.

"I know." Well that's annoying.

"Wait a minute. How is this going to help us?" Are we going to mail him home?

"Well as soon as we can figure out where Leonard lives"

"I know where I live," Leonard interrupts Amy's plan. Leonard has been sitting so quietly that I almost forgot how annoying he is.

Amy patiently looks at Leonard and gives him a quick but genuine smile. She then continues, "After we have Leonard's address you can give him a ride home."

"I said I know where I live." Amy can only keep up this polite demeanor so long and I can feel it slowly wearing away.

"You may know where you live Leonard but you don't know your address or how to get home."

"I know how to get home."

"Okay then pal, why don't you get out of here

174

then." I head towards the front door while saying this.

"It is far too late for you to be walking home alone Leonard. Mitchell you are going to give him a ride when we get his address off of his envelope." She says this pithily, much of the politeness worn away.

I stop at the door contemplating opening it anyway. Show this kid who's boss. As I have made the decision to open the door I hear Amy sigh in desperation and I quickly undecide to open the door.

"I can't find your envelope Leonard. Did you put it in your pocket or maybe drop it somewhere other than the 'thank you' box?"

"My mom didn't give me an envelope." I'd like to remind him that she didn't give him a card to go with his toy truck either but I think Amy would bite my head off at this point.

"No, no, when she came in the box was right on the table. She couldn't have missed it; I moved that table by the door so no one could miss it."

"My mom didn't come in, don't you remember? She dropped me off." Leonard says while standing up.

"Obviously not Leonard," I answer for Amy.

"Well what are you doing?" Amy is referring to his sudden rise from the chair.

"I'm going to go home now, I'm bored."

This is my cue and I open the door wide and smile. "Goodnight Leonard. Please be careful and walk directly home."

"No! I said it is too late to be walking home alone. It's quarter past nine for crying out loud." Rarely do I see Amy this pissed off. I am kind of enjoying it. At least I am at the moment but this won't be pretty later on after we finally get rid of this kid. By some means this will turn into my fault.

"Well Amy, what should we do? This wasn't supposed to be a slumber party."

"Don't tell me what this party was supposed to be. I am the one who planned it. All by myself I might add." Here we go. I knew this would swing around to be my fault but I didn't expect it to happen so quickly.

"And you did a wonderful job. It was a fantastic party." I am building in sarcasm, "So much fun that the guests just don't want to leave."

"Actually I do want to leave," Leonard butts in saving me from myself, "and I know how to get home on my own so get out of my way."

I gladly move to the side until Amy gives me a fierce look that actually scares me. I quickly move back in front of the door just in time, or maybe a tad too late because I collide with Leonard and knock him over. "Sorry about that

Leonard. Get up and I'll give you a ride home. I'll drive and you can tell me how to get there." I conceal the fact that I really, and I mean really, enjoyed knocking him over.

"Whatever," he grumbles while standing up.

"I'll start cleaning up and we can talk when you get back." She doesn't even look at me when she says this. Just like that, she is out of the kitchen and out of sight.

"Whatever," I say taking a line from Leonard.

"Excuse me!" Out of the room, and out of sight, but not out of earshot.

"Come on Leonard let's get you home."

We are walking silently to the car while I am wondering how much trouble I am going to be in when I get home. I consider stopping on the way home to buy some flowers but I wouldn't even know where to stop this late at night. She wouldn't even appreciate the cheap bouquets from Nowak's. No, she only likes the big expensive bouquets from the florist over on McKinley Parkway. We get to the car and he opens the front passenger door.

"Actually you have to sit in the back Leonard," I say while slipping behind the wheel.

"Just take me home," he retorts while flopping into the front seat.

"Do you think this is some kind of joke? Move your ass to the back seat!"

"No!" With that he slams the front door closed with the strength of a boy twice his size.

"If you don't get into the back seat we aren't going to be going anywhere Leonard." I'm the adult here. I say what goes.

"I don't care. I'll just walk home."

I know that Amy will kill me if I let him walk home. On the other hand, if I let him walk home and then pulled out of the driveway to circle the neighborhood a couple of times I could get rid of this pain in the ass kid and get some alone time before heading back into the house to get reamed.

"Did you hear me? I said I'll walk home."

"Yeah, yeah I heard you." I figure it's only a couple of blocks so I lean over and open the door for him.

I didn't think he was bluffing but if there was any doubt it has now gone out the passenger door along with him. As I am about to pull out of the driveway myself a pair of headlights pulls in behind me. Shit!

I hop out of the car to see Leonard walking toward the newly arrived car. He wasn't even a full house away so I am hoping that he will just hop in the beat up car and head off without a word. Those thoughts of a quiet exit are smashed when I hear the front door open and see Amy approaching with an envelope and a pen in one hand while waving with the other.

"Let's just let them go honey, it's late." I say this while scrambling out of my seat but a woman has already emerged from the driver side of the car. I can tell by her build that she is rather young, probably in her twenties, but her features look like that of a thirty or even forty year old woman. I guess having a son like Leonard would age anyone beyond their years.

"Be quiet," is all that Amy speaks to my suggestion.

"What's the big idea here?" The older looking young lady demands while looking right past Amy to yours truly.

"How do you mean?" Amy who is older but looks much younger says in response.

"I mean that I am barely twenty minutes late and you just send my boy packing?"

"Well there must be some miscommunication ma'am."

"Then by all means explain for me," the younger older lady cuts in.

"Thank you, I will. You see the party actually ended three hours and twenty minutes ago and my husband and I called your house several times."

"I wasn't home," again cutting in.

"Yes, we gathered as much. So we looked through

our 'thank you' box full of return addressed envelopes until we realized that you have yet to fill one out. I brought one out for you by the way. Anyway, once we realized that we didn't have your address Leonard informed us that he could tell us how to get home so my husband Mitchell," she points to me and I just nod hoping not to be found out, "was about to drive him home when you pulled in."

"That sure as hell isn't what it looked like to me."

I'm screwed.

"Well what did it look like?" Amy is perplexed but I am sure that she won't be for long.

"When I pulled up my boy was walking half way down the block, in the wrong direction I might add, all alone." He wasn't half way down the block but I figure that it is better to keep all the details to myself for the time being.

"That can't be," Amy says this as she looks at me and is clearly waiting for my interjection.

"I was just waiting for Leonard to move to the back seat. You see, he started by sitting in the front but I know that is not the safest place for a child so I asked him to move to the back. He was just simply moving to the back seat." Bullshit. I know it and they know it.

"Well where in the hell were you off to when I pulled in?"

"He was taking Leonard to your home." Amy

simultaneously says this as a statement to young old lady while posing it as a question to me.

"Bullshit," says young old lady, and she is exactly right. "He was pulling out with only himself in the car and Leonard was half way down the street walking away from the car." It still is not the time to say so but he wasn't half way down the street. One house at the most.

Amy who is always clear minded in tough situations has figured out, more or less, what has happened and changes gears. "I apologize for any miscommunications or folly on our part. Leonard was a wonderful guest and we were pleased to spend the extra time with him. We hope that we can arrange a play date in the near future between your sweet Leonard and our Leslie."

To this she receives a blank stare. Apparently young old lady does not know where to take this conversation next so Amy continues.

"I know that it is getting late but if you wouldn't mind filling out this envelope with your address before you get Leonard home for bed." She extends the envelope and pen in the young old lady's direction.

There is a pause that seems like forever until she finally moves towards her car and says, "Stick that pen up your ass. The envelope too!"

Amy doesn't say a word as she watches Leonard

join his mother in the car, in the front seat I might add, and they back out of the driveway. She stands frozen and waits for them to pull away.

I too am frozen, paralyzed in fear of my own wife.

"Mitchell, what the hell just happened?"

"Just a big misunderstanding Amy. I am going to go and get some milk and when I get home I will explain the entire thing." I make a move toward the handle on the car door.

"Get your ass in the house right now." Rarely does Amy use words so strongly. "You have from this spot to the kitchen to figure out your story and I suggest that you strongly consider the truth."

My mind is a tornado of thought as I begin my trek toward the kitchen.

TWELVE

September 17, 1990

"Forgive me Father for I have sinned." It's Mrs. McCabe, I can tell by the voice.

"How long has it been since your last confession my dear?" It's been one week.

"It has been seven days Father."

"And what are your confessions my dear?" I could name them for her at this point. She comes in every week with the same trio of sins. She doesn't like her daughter in law, she resents people who view the Catholic Church with contempt, and she needles her husband about odd jobs.

"Well father I had a disagreement with my son over how he and his wife discipline their son."

Check. "Go on my dear."

"I engaged in a heated argument with a lady from my book club about the Eucharist. Mind you that I didn't say anything that I regret or that I would take back but I wish I could have used a different tone."

Check two. "Continue my dear."

"I chastised my husband for not starting a job on time this weekend."

Check final. "What job would that be my dear?" It was the job of painting the outside of the house. I know this because last week she 'chastised' her husband for not purchasing the correct shade of blue paint for their house that he would be painting this weekend.

If I know Mr. McCabe, and I do, he will be painting the entire house himself this weekend. He'll get most of it done while his wife is here complaining to me about him not getting up on time to begin. Never mind the fact that he must be nearing seventy years old and will no doubt be needing to climb an extension ladder to reach the second story of the house.

"He is painting the house this weekend Father."

"Okay my dear. Is that all for today?"

"Yes Father. For these and all the sins of my past life, especially for my sins of which we spoke here today I am truly sorry."

"My dear, remember to pray for your son and his family. It is okay to discuss your beliefs with others but please do remember that your words and demeanor reflect on the Catholic Church as a whole. Thank God for your husband and appreciate his deeds."

"Yes Father."

"Say two Hail Mary's, three Our Father's, one Act of Confession, and then go home and tell your husband that you appreciate him. Now please say the act of Contrition."

"Oh My God, I am heartily sorry…"

As Mrs. McCabe goes on I think how odd it is that she comes every week with the same sins in a different variation. Of course each week she comes in and receives absolution from the prior week's sins. Then off she goes to collect the same satchel of sins, only to return here in a week's time and empty them again.

How much simpler it would be for Mrs. McCabe if she would just leave her son and his family be. They are here each Sunday at Mass and seem like a fine family. Just that one act would lighten her load tremendously. I want to sit here and dissect other possibilities to reduce Mrs. McCabe's guilt but I am aware of the silence in the Confessional.

"You are absolved of your sins my dear."

"Thank You Father." Out she goes to say her penance. From there she will light a few candles for her son and his family. She will light a few more for family members that have passed on to God's Kingdom. Finally she will head home and wait for her husband to descend from his ladder and thank her husband for painting the house. I can only hope that she will be compelled to throw in a hug and kiss to show her appreciation for the good man.

I am rather surprised at how quickly I hear the Confessional door open and close. I sometimes sit here uninterrupted for ten to fifteen minutes. There are the usual ladies who come in promptly at ten o'clock; Mrs. O'Donnell, Mrs. Clark, and Mrs. McCabe. Always in that order unless one is missing, which is very rare. They begin waiting for me as soon as nine o'clock Mass ends, which they attend faithfully. After that though, it is a scattering of ladies who show up once a month in some random order until I begin Noon Mass.

I very rarely encounter a woman that I do not recognize by voice alone, nor do I have many men looking for absolution from their sins. The few men that I do hear tend to disappear directly after Mass during the football season, if they attend at all.

"Bless me Father for I have sinned but that is not what I am here to talk about." Mrs. Kingston, I can tell not only by the voice but by the lack of reverence for my position. She babysat me a handful of times when I was a boy so she continues to treat me like a child.

"Yes my dear what is on your mind?"

"Look Ben, I really need to know how things have been going with Leonard."

"Mrs. Kingston, please call me 'Father Ben' and I have told you before that I cannot discuss what, if anything, Leonard and I talk about together." That boy never shows up at this church unless he is with her.

"What do you mean by 'if anything'? Has he not been showing up?"

"Mrs. Kingston if you can arrange for that boy to be here Sunday mornings then I will be more than happy to put him to work around the Parrish."

"He has been here the last two weeks and I still haven't seen him as an Alter boy." And you never will.

"He hasn't shown to the alter boy learning lessons, nor has he shown in any other capacity unless he is accompanied by you Mrs. Kingston."

"Well that just can't be. He has been sitting quietly in the back of the church waiting for me the last two weeks. When I get here he tells me how much he has learned from you and it is only a short time before he is assisting you with Mass."

"I regret to inform you that I have had no dialogue with the boy since the last time we spoke, us three." I probably shouldn't be telling her all of this information but I am hoping it will help Leonard out. He has had a very tough go of it lately.

"Well he is here now and I will be leaving him with

187

you until I come back for five o'clock Mass."

I believe that I hear her stand up and open the door. I am sure that this is what I have heard because I also hear the door close behind her. I panic and step out of my side of the Confessional.

"Mrs. Kingston," I whisper as loudly as I can while walking after her. She is moving quickly because by the time I am close enough for her to stop we are already passed Leonard who is sitting in the last pew. We are in the back of the church next to the exit and approximately five feet from Leonard.

"Father Ben I have been coming here since before you were born and when I was a girl Father Jude spent all of his free time working with troubled boys from the neighborhood. I remember my very own cousin James spending many Sundays with him."

"Yes, Father Jude was a wonderful man." She begins speaking again before I can continue my spiel.

"You know my cousin James don't you?"

"Yes Mrs. Kingston."

"Of course you do because he is here every Sunday at five o'clock Mass with his beautiful family. He is here at five o'clock because he is a hard working man and picks up an extra morning shift on Sundays so he can provide anything that his beautiful wife or two wonderful daughters need from him."

"He is a tremendous parishioner Mrs. Kingston." Again she cuts in before I can go any further.

"I do believe that extra shift helps him to put some money in the basket as well, doesn't it Father Ben?" She stops and looks to me for a reply.

"Yes Mrs. Kingston I believe it does." I don't even try to go on because I can tell that she is not finished and won't allow it.

"Well if it weren't for Father Jude my wonderful cousin James who provides for his family, shows up faithfully every Sunday at five o'clock, and drops a few dollars into your basket would be in jail or at least a general derelict in our community."

"I see your point Mrs. Kingston." I wasn't finished.

"Good! I am glad. God Bless you Father Ben, you are a good man." Before I have a chance to say anything else she has opened the door and manages to leave me in a state of shock and mild contemplation.

I turn around and survey the scene. There are no more people waiting outside the confessional so I am good on that front. I look at the clock and see that I only have five minutes or so before noon Mass is to start. I see Mark and Matthew Boyle, the Alter boys for this Mass. They are fine young men and are already making their way to the back of the church for the procession.

The church is roughly half full and will be three quarters full by the time I start, when all of the last minute arrivals are here. It always surprises me to see how many more seats are full once I reach the Alter and turn around from the procession. It's almost as if they were already crouched down in their pews and they pop up just as I am about to turn and face the parishioners.

"Leonard," I say as I approach the last pew, "when Mass has ended we will get to work tiding up the church."

"I want to clean the organ." Rather forward of the boy.

"You can clean the organ next week if you arrive earlier. I am sure that Mrs. Smith will enjoy the company."

"I want to clean it today."

"You can clean it if you arrive earlier next week Leonard. Mrs. Smith is no longer here and she is the only one allowed to touch the organ. She is only here for the early services." She is a wonderful organist but she can only be here for the seven thirty and the nine o'clock Masses. She charges us no money so we can hardly complain. She does make exceptions if the Bishop or a high-ranking member of the archdiocese will be attending a later Mass.

"I don't need no Mrs. Smith to clean the organ." I don't like all of this back talk or his dry little smile but Mass is just about to begin and I can't keep everyone else waiting because I am arguing with a twelve year old.

"Leonard when I am finished with Mass we will take a butter knife and go around and remove all of the gum from beneath the pews. You wouldn't believe how many little boys think that beneath a pew is a good place to stick their gum prior to receiving the Body and Blood of Christ."

Now it's my turn for a dry little smile because I saw Leonard do this just last week. I witnessed Mrs. Kingston say something to Leonard; I deduced that it was to swallow his gum because he went on to make a big act of swallowing it and pretending to choke. To this he received a mighty back slap from Mrs. Kingston, I believe it was to help him with the choking but I would bet that old Mrs. Kingston wanted to whack him one just because. I could tell that the people surrounding him did. Once Mrs. Kingston stood up to exit the pew, her head bowed, I watched him take the gum out from under his tongue and stick it beneath the pew in front of him. I do believe that I will have him begin with that pew.

"I'll see you after Mass Leonard." No reply. In fact he turns around in his pew, grabs a hymnal, and opens it up just to confirm his disinterest in me.

"Father it is time for Mass," says Mark. Mark is the

older Boyle boy by a year and a half. He is a very responsible thirteen-year-old boy and I hope that I don't lose him. Alter boys have a way of disappearing around the age of adolescence. They are preoccupied with sports, dating, and beer.

"Thank you," I nod in appreciation toward Mark. "Let us begin," I direct this at both Mark and Matthew, the younger Boyle boy.

Matthew is a bit more playful than Mark but in no way does this mean he is troublesome. He can often be found at the baseball diamond working on his throwing arm. I guess that's how it goes for the younger brother; Mark gets to be the big hitter while Matthew is stuck throwing pitches and shagging balls. God has a funny way of working things out though. Mark was the best pitcher on the St. Clare baseball team in the Catholic grammar school league last year. Many people overlooked this because they were transfixed on the amount of homeruns Mark was hitting; he ended the season only two shy of the grammar school single season record. Now that he's heading to high school I am confident that Matthew will receive his time to shine.

The bells ring and the clergy stands. As I am heading down the isle I am disappointed by the turnout. It seems that the later in the day that the Mass occurs the more available seats there are. I wish that the Holiday Catholics could see this now. Those folks who show up only on Easter and Christmas Eve to complain that there isn't enough seating would be singing a different tune today. The same folks who fawn over the good old days of Father Jude, as if they attended Mass more often when he was here. They didn't.

I see familiar faces as I approach the front of the church; Mrs. O'Donnell, Mrs. Clark, and Mrs. McCabe. They are here every Sunday for nine o'clock Mass, Confession, followed by the noon Mass. Then they go out together for lunch, which they always invite me to but I never attend.

I am so busy cleaning up from the earlier services and then preparing for the evening five o'clock Mass that I just don't have the time. I do hope to take them up on their offer one of these days. They have been so supportive of me since I was assigned this parish, nearly three years ago now. It is a shame that their families no longer attend with them. Occasionally they will bring a child or grandchild but unless it's a holiday you won't be seeing any of their husbands sitting next to them. A shame, I say.

The processional has finished and as I turn I take a visual scan of the congregation. As anticipated there are more people in pews now than just a short walk ago. I would say that for every step that I took one person entered the church. I took roughly forty steps. Even with the additional tardies the church is still more than a quarter empty. I am sure that Father Jude took in the same view many a Sunday afternoon; just don't try to tell that to anybody here.

There is one seat that is noticeably empty. It isn't one of the front pews; those are always filled with Mrs. O'Donnell, Mrs. Clark, Mrs. McCabe and the like. The middle pews are always very spotty, like looking at a third grade classroom during flu season. The last few pews are generally very hard seats to come by unless you are here early. I often wonder why these seats are such a commodity. I suppose they're made up of all of the people that will be ready to leave as quickly as possible, often not even returning to their seats after the Communion. Whatever seats in the back remain will surely be populated by the many late arrivals.

However, one seat is wide open in the back of the church. It was the seat formally inhabited by Leonard. I expected him to be trouble for me today but I didn't expect him to leave. I suppose that he figured that he would have more fun playing with his friends than he would spending time cleaning the church with me. I suppose he is right. Poor Mrs. Kingston, she will be furious when she hears this.

I recognize that Mrs. Kingston will have to wait because the congregation is ready to sit so I must open the Mass.

As I am opening my mouth to begin the Mass I hear the most appalling and unpleasant noise. It is coming from high above and it is coming from the organ.

THIRTEEN

July 31, 1991

"Come on in here."

I know what he is thinking. "No Leonard. Get out of there right now." He is sitting on their bed.

"Come on Cindy just for a minute. It's really comfortable; I think it's a water bed."

"Seriously Leonard get out of there before you mess up their bed and I have to try and make it back to where they won't notice." You can never make someone else's bed in the same manner that they do. It's impossible.

"I think that we should mess up their bed just a little bit anyway babe." He has that never give up smile on his face again.

"Come on Leonard please get out of there I don't want to make up the bed." I plead with him hoping that he can see that there will be no kissing if he doesn't get out of there.

"Fine," he sighs and gets up. He must have realized

that there would be no making out if he didn't get up.

I like making out with Leonard, his kisses are extremely passionate. Right now we only kiss and little more but I think I might let him go a little further soon; we have been dating for the entire summer. Some of the girls at school don't like Leonard because he is always getting into trouble and sent out of the classroom but I think that he is fun. He just needs a little work.

"Let's hit the couch." He says this as he brushes by me.

"I think that you better leave Leonard. It's almost eight o'clock and they could be home any minute." I don't want him to really leave. I just want him to tell me that he wants to stay longer, besides they are rarely home before ten o'clock on the weekend anyway.

"Come on babe you know that they aren't going to be home for a couple of more hours." He plops down on the leather couch in the living room but doesn't turn on the television. Instead he looks at me and croons, "besides I want to spend a little more time with you. Over here on the couch though."

He pats the spot he would like me to sit on with his hand. It is on the left side of him. He does this on purpose because he is always trying to undo my bra with his right hand. I used to stop him but it turns out that he is actually very gentle. I was surprised because he kisses so aggressively. Unfortunately he tries to get it off every time we are together now, even if I just want to kiss.

"Okay but just a little longer," I say as I take the seat situated to the right of him and his pesky bra hand. Leonard is the first boy that I ever let take off my bra and he is the first boy that I ever put my hands into his pants. I won't let him put his hand down mine though. I don't want to get pregnant like my sister. She had a baby and now my parents are too busy raising her son to spend any time with me, especially my dad. He always wanted a boy anyway.

"Let's make ourselves more comfortable," Leonard says as he stands up, crosses in front of me, and sits back down on the other side of me.

"Not too comfortable. I don't want Richard to hear us."

"You're worried about a six year old?" Leonard says as he chuckles, leans in, and plants his lips partially on mine and partially on my cheek.

I am lured in only momentarily before I pull back and say, "I am worried about him seeing us and telling his folks. Then I'll be out of a job."

"That will just give us more time together baby." Each word he says is closer to my face until he punctuates with another intense kiss.

I let this one linger a little longer before again pulling back and saying, "We spend a lot of time together baby." I want him to tell me that he likes it and wants more time with me.

"It's never enough," he whispers and begins to kiss my neck. I am wrapped in his kisses when I feel that hand reach around under my shirt.

"Come on Leonard seriously I don't want to wake Richard and get canned." If only we were at Leonard's apartment we could take this further. No one is ever at Leonard's place and even on the rare occurrence that his mom is home she doesn't care what we do. She can tell we are in love.

"Why not? I say we leave right now and head to my place. My mom is out and we can have the place to ourselves." He is looking at me and I can tell he is serious.

"No baby, I can't."

"Tell me why?"

"I told you before that I can't quit because I need the money. Ever since my folks started raising my nephew there is no more extra money for me." I like to have a few extra dollars so that I can take the bus into the city and shop for things. I love going into the city. It's not New York City or Paris, from what I can tell from the photographs, but there are wonderful shops in Buffalo brimming with shoes, jewelry, and purses. There are also cute little coffee shops that I can sit at with a fancy cup of coffee and, depending on who is working the counter, have a smoke.

"So you can buy purses and shoes? I say you quit so we can go back to my place and spend our nights kissing and…" he stops there and throws me a wink.

"Then who would buy your cigarettes?"

"I was smoking long before I met you babe," he says while sitting back into the couch with a huff.

He seems a little pissed off so I soften my tone and say, "Baby you know I want to spend all my time smooching you but I really need this job." Then I lean over to him and fix a big kiss on his cheek.

He looks at me and I can tell that he is over his little pouty party and that he is ready to go again. He leans in and begins to kiss me forcefully. He has his left hand on the back of my head and is exploring the inside of my mouth with his tongue. I can taste the stale smoke on his breath and smell it on his shirt and it makes me tingle all over. His right hand begins to unsnap my bra and I put up a small fight, just for show. His hand has moved its way to the front of my shirt in an attempt to lift it up and possibly over my head. I grab his hand tightly so he is aware that I don't want any of my skin exposed in case Richard comes down. He seems to get the point and begins a firm message of my breasts. They aren't large but they are there, which is more than I can say for most of the girls my age. He starts to pinch my nipples and it hurts but oddly enough I don't want him to stop. Then all of a sudden I do want him to stop. I think I heard a noise coming from upstairs.

"Hold on," I gasp as I pull back and try to listen for sounds of movement.

"Can't," he replies as he continues to maul at me.

"Seriously hold on Leonard." I try to say this firmly without upsetting him.

He simply points to the bulge being retained by his jeans and restates, "Can't."

I want so badly to reach my hand down into those pants and grab a hold of his hard penis. I want to caress it and know that it is responding to my touch. I want to feel Leonard shudder and hope that he tells me again that he loves me as he did the first time my hands were fishing in his pants. Instead I stand up fasten my bra and give him a kiss and say, "I'll be right back, I am going to check on Richard."

I can feel how badly he needs me as I am leaving the room. I look over to him as I ascend the stairs and I can see in his face that he wants me. I smile and gaze at him until he is out of sight. I then focus my attention on Richard's door. It looks like it is cracked to just about the same spot that I had left it at after tucking him into bed.

He is most likely fast asleep; he rarely gives me any trouble at all. He is a sweet boy and his parents are very good to him. They always bring him something from their evenings out and they place it next to his bed for him to discover when he awakens.

Sometimes when I am here alone after he has fallen asleep I lie in their guest bedroom and pretend that it is my room, in my house, and that Richard's lovely parents are mine also. I picture them coming home with hugs, kisses, and a present for me.

I am snapped out of my daydream about my daydream because I am sure that I have heard something in Richard's room.

"Richard honey," I say softly as I gently open the door to his room and enter.

"Go away," a pile of blankets, pillows, and stuffed bears says to me.

"Richard honey, what's wrong?" I try to use a soothing voice incase he has had a bad dream.

"Go away." I have caught him with a flashlight and comic book inside his blanket fortress before but he usually just pretends to be asleep when I call him.

"What's the matter Richard?"

"No. Go away. I mean it. Get out of here." A

tirade of pleas and I don't know what to do. So I press on.

"Richard, my little man, please tell me what is the matter?"

"You wouldn't understand."

"I bet I would if you would just tell me honey." I move closer to the bed.

"No you wouldn't now go away."

"Try me." I sit down on the edge of his bed.

The pile of plush shifts and his head emerges. His eyes are swollen and wet with tears. His cheeks are bright red in embarrassment, but over what? As I am wondering Richard has a request, "Promise that you won't laugh at me?"

"I promise Richard."

He shoves the crumbled fort to the ground and reveals that he has urinated all over himself and his bed.

"Well that's no problem. Just throw your clothes and sheets in the hamper while I go and run you a bath. While you are in the bath I will put clean sheets on your bed. After that you can get some shut eye before your parents even get home."

"Thanks Cindy."

"No problem honey."

On the way out of the room I think it will be a better idea to go and tell Leonard to get out of here before starting the water but one step past the bathroom I turn back and re-order my plan. I don't want Richard to come looking for me and find Leonard so I turn on the hot water. After the water turns from cold to hot, which doesn't take too long in July, I turn the cold knob half way and plug the drain.

On my way out of the bathroom I nearly bump into Richard. He is stark naked and has as many freckles on his butt as he does his face. I find this cute and smile warmly at him before saying, "Okay honey hop in and I'll be up in three minutes to check on you."

"Okay," he says while nodding his head.

"Let's keep this quick so we can have you back in bed before your mom and dad get home." I'm not sure if he has heard me over the water and because we are both moving in different directions.

As I get to the bottom of the stairs I don't see Leonard on the couch. I walk over to it and lean over the back to see if he is lying down. Not there. I start towards the bedroom thinking he has gotten his bravado back up and thinks I might want to move in there with him. I find him on my way to the bedroom. He is sitting in the kitchen with a glass that is a quarter full of a clear liquid. I know my Leonard well enough to know that it isn't an innocent glass of water.

"What are you doing?" I say with mock horror.

"I'm Relaxing. Would you like me to pour you one?" He says reaching for the vodka bottle that sits in front of him. I look to the liquor cabinet's simple lock that has been jimmied open again.

"No, actually I don't, and you can't have anymore."

"And why is that?"

"For one, because you have watered that bottle down so many times that I can't imagine there is any booze left in there anyway."

"They'll never know. They probably mix it with juice or something so they can't taste the alcohol anyway. In a way I'm doing them a favor, if you look at it that way."

"Okay then, for two, because Richard is awake and taking a bath."

"A bath?"

"Yes Leonard, a bath, and now I have some work to do and his parents will be home soon so please leave. I'll call you when I get home."

"So because he shit himself you're kicking me out?" He says with his voice raised.

"He didn't shit himself and I'm not kicking you out." I say quietly hoping he follows suit.

"Okay sorry," he says this with extreme sarcasm but he has quieted down. "So because he pissed the bed you're kicking me out." Again he uses the raised voice.

"It's not like that Leonard." He is twisting this all around.

"Not like what?" I am taken aback by his booming question. Leonard tends to be loud but for some reason he is louder than I have ever heard him before.

"It's not like you are making it out to be."

"How am I making it out to be?"

"I don't know Leonard. All I know is that I am Richard's baby sitter and right now he needs me to change his sheets and start some laundry." While I am saying this he finishes his glass of watered down vodka and pours out another half glass.

"Well you run a long. I'll be right here waiting." He says rather indignantly.

I know that I don't have much longer to argue. The tub must be near full and Richard will soon turn off the faucets. When he does there will be nothing but standing air between Leonard's intense voice and his little ears. He knows not to close the bathroom door while he is in the tub so that I can keep my ears on him.

"Go on!" Leonard shouts sensing my inner hesitation.

"I'll be right back." I say while walking backward toward the staircase. Half of me would like him to stay so we can work this out when I get back. The other half of me wants him to leave because he is being so boisterous and I don't want Richard to hear him.

When I walk into the bathroom I immediately see that I came just in time because the water has risen to the tub's capacity. Richard has yet to notice because he is so entranced in his pirate fantasy. He has on an eye patch and has brought a plastic sword into the bathtub with him. He is in the midst of slaying a ship made from an egg carton when I walk in.

"Okay Richard it looks like you are more than clean. I am going to turn off the water and pull the plug. When the tub is empty I want you to dry off and go back to your room."

He smiles at me and his eyes, rather his un-patched eye, seem appreciative. I smile outwardly as well as inwardly as I leave to make up his bed. As quickly as my face returns from the smile, my ears hear Leonard making a terrible racket. I tell myself that Richard won't hear anything with all the water gurgling down the drain but it is hard for me to ignore.

I race to the linen closet and grab a clean sheet adorned with a cartoon character that I am not familiar with. I hastily put the new sheet over the mattress ignoring the still damp urine circle on the bed. I am barely exiting

Richard's room when I hear his voice.

"I'm out of here." It's Leonard. He sounds calm.

"Okay. I'll call your house when I get home." I try to sound loving.

"Don't bother, I won't be there."

"Where will you be?" I try not to sound panicky as I pass the bathroom and approach the steps.

"Don't worry about it. I'll get a hold of you when I'm free." He still sounds calm but in a measured way.

"Well where will you be Leonard?" The words are interrupted by the sound of the front door closing as I reach the stairs. I finish my thought anyway, "and with whom?"

"Who are you talking to?" I spin around to see Richard in a towel with his hair still wet.

"The pizza guy," I say hastily. "Now dry your hair and climb back into bed honey." I try to sound unflustered.

"There's pizza?" His face lights up.

"No there is no pizza. It was the wrong address or a prank by one of the neighbors. Now if I'm not mistaken your parents will be home shortly so off to bed with you." I don't think his parents will actually be home for another hour but I don't want him asking anymore questions.

"Okay. Goodnight Cindy." He hops like a frog toward his room leaving a trail of water as he goes.

"Please dry yourself off better before you get back

into bed Richard," I say to silence as I head back down toward the kitchen to see if Leonard has cleaned up after himself before his exit. I doubt it.

As I am walking down the stairs and through the living room in the direction of the kitchen I am wondering where Leonard is off to and who he is going to be with. I worry that he is going to end up with one of those fast moving girls like Stacey or Heather. Or even worse, he might go and spend time with that ex-girlfriend of his; Beth. She's such trash.

All of those thoughts leave my head as I enter the kitchen and lay my eyes on what has happened. What he has apparently done. The bottle of vodka is missing; however that is the least of my concerns. There is an empty bottle of red wine on the counter top near the sink. The contents of that bottle have been poured throughout the kitchen. I follow the trail around the kitchen, being careful not to step in it, and realize that it has not touched anywhere where it can leave a stain. It is chiefly on the tiled floor but the trail does climb up onto a chair and finish in the center of the dinner table.

That jerk. That asshole. That prick. How could he tell me that he loves me and then do something like this to me?

I am trying to focus on hating Leonard when I

realize that this needs to be cleaned up quickly. I don't know what I am going to say about the missing bottles of vodka and red wine but hopefully they won't notice because they have a massive liquor cabinet that seems to go largely untouched.

I grab a roll of paper towels and hit my hands and knees to begin scrubbing. It is a fierce battle between the paper towels and the strong red wine. It seems to take nearly three paper towels for each tile. At this rate it will take me thirty minutes or more to clean up.

While cleaning my anger starts to subside. I start to see things from Leonard's point of view. He was frustrated with me because I, the woman that he loves, invited him over so that we could spend some alone time together after Richard went to bed. Instead I spend half the night telling him what to do and what not to do and the other half of the night ignoring him for Richard.

When the job is about half done I realize that I need to make this up to my man. I know exactly how to do it too. I decide that I will give him my virginity. I mean why not? I love him and he loves me. I don't want to lose him to one of those trampy girls he hangs around with. Lord knows they are willing to give it up.

I am picturing how beautiful it will be and how happy it will make him when he finds out about my decision, when suddenly I hear the front door open. I guess I won't have to wait after all.

I am sure he has come back to help me clean up and apologize, although he has no reason to apologize. We will be so happy together from here on out.

"Cindy."

Oh no!

"We're home a little early."

FOURTEEN
March 12, 1992

"Now just hold it right there," I command as I spot his coat dart behind a shed. It's not a good idea to wear a bright red coat if you plan on robbing somebody's house.

"I didn't do anything," is all that comes from behind the shed. Unlikely since I just received a call for a breaking and entering that matches his description. It is generally a sure sign of guilt when a suspect takes off running the instant that they see a squad car approach.

"Then come on out here so we can clear up this mess." I will give him a minute before I start to move in. He is behind a shed that is tight up against a wooden fence that is approximately six feet high.

We have already been running for about two minutes, which doesn't sound like a long time but I would say that we have covered a quarter mile and hopped three fences. When I think of how easily he hopped those fences, almost as easily as me, I rethink waiting on him and head toward the shed.

"Okay I'm coming out." The actual words fly right in one ear and out of the other. What catches my attention is that the words sound labored as if he is struggling with a task. I round the corner of the peeling blue shed to see only from his ass down, the remainder of him has already folded over the fence.

"Hold it right there!" I lunge and grab a hold of his left foot at the very last moment before I am stuck looking at nothing more than a cherry stained fence. I start to climb the fence myself when I hear a thud and the weight of the foot I am holding lightens tremendously. There is a reason for that; I am left with nothing more than a shoe in my hand.

I scale and hop over the remainder of the fence rather quickly and hurl the shoe at the male who is running away from me as I again begin chase. I figure that he is probably in his early teens by his build and voice. I didn't get a good look at his face but from what I did see he is a Caucasian. His voice sounded vaguely familiar but not recognizable enough for me to place.

As I am chasing him I tell myself just to keep a good pace because he has youth on his side; I don't want to shoot the moon and run out of gas. However I have a great deal on my side; it's still cold enough outside that there are patches of snow which should bother his shoeless foot, we are traipsing through backyards strewn with toys discarded when dinner was ready or a favorite television show came on, and every five or six yards we will come to a fence to hop. Not to mention that they don't call me 'fast Eddy' for nothing.

The chase continues on for a minute or so more and only encounters one additional fence, which he clears shoddily. It is merely one of those generic four-foot chain link fences and I hop it with the aide of only one hand. I nearly slip on the landing but regain my form in time to watch the perpetrator slip and fall face first into a sandbox.

As I approach him I realize that he must have smashed his face on the side of it because there is already a pool of blood forming in the sandbox. His breathing is labored but I figure that's from the chase and not the fall.

I give him a mild poke with my foot and ask, "You hurt?" I don't want to touch him because of the blood. Besides, it's rather apparent that he isn't going to be going anywhere.

"Is everything okay out here officer?" I turn to see a husky man emerging from his back door. He is typical of this neighborhood. His size and appearance indicate that he is most likely a laborer, probably an ironworker or a garbage man. It is legitimate to assume that he works hard enough to keep his job but not hard enough to want to quit. His build suggests that he likes his wife's home cooked meals as well as a couple of beers after work. This neighborhood is full of hard working people who don't need some punk kid robbing them and then leading chases through their backyards.

"Everything will be fine sir. I am going to have to ask you to head back inside. I will come and speak with you in a moment, once my backup arrives." I give him a nod and he heads back inside of his house. I notice that the upstairs window has a face in it and I give a wave and thumbs up so they won't be worried. The face doesn't acknowledge me and I am sure that the face in the window will shortly be joined by another face, if not more.

I hear a moaning which reminds me to leave the window people alone and deal with the criminal lying face down in the sandbox.

"Roll over," I direct him while assisting his role with my foot rather firmly.

"Ugh," is all he can manage as he flops over.

"Well, well, well, if it isn't my dear friend." I am sure even in his state he can pick up on the mockery in my voice.

"Hello officer." He says with his own brand of mockery.

"What have I been telling you?" I have been busting this kid for crimes for the last five or six years. His offenses grow more mature with his age. "Well, what have I been telling you and your nit wit friends?"

I wait a few seconds for an answer. He is still breathing heavy but it looks like the bleeding has stopped. I can't be sure but it appears to be nothing more than a nose bleed. At worst he broke his nose. He usually has some smart ass reply whenever I speak with him. In an attempt to ignore me he tries to roll back over.

I place my foot squarely on his chest and apply moderate pressure before asking again, "What have I been saying to you for the last few years Lenny?"

Again all he can manage is, "Ugh."

While applying a great deal more pressure I say, "Lenny, I want an answer."

"I can't answer with you stomping the life out of me."

"First Lenny, this is not stomping." I pick up my foot and bring it back down swiftly and squarely on his chest. "That was stomping and if you don't answer me you will get a whole lot more of it. Second, I want you to tell me what I have been saying to you time and time again." My foot is pushing down again on his chest.

"Okay, okay," he gasps and goes on, "If we don't

cut it out you'll be arresting us for a serious crime."

"And look where we are now; you being arrested for breaking and entering after running from the police. I told you that this was going to happen to you Lenny. I tried to warn you over and over."

"I can't believe I got caught by fast Eddy; the guys are going to rip me apart." I sense a great deal of sarcasm in his voice when he says my name.

"Well, that's what happens when you try to run on foot from the fastest cop on the beat, Lenny."

"Are you kidding me?" He begins to laugh as he continues on, "You think you're fast?" His laughter has subsided but he continues, "We call you 'fast Eddy' because you spend all your time chasing kids out of the golf course when they are drinking on the greens. The only ones you ever catch are either hammered or girls."

"Which one are you?" I enjoy watching his smile fade as the question sinks in.

I decide that it's time to remove my foot from his chest. He sits up and wipes the blood from his nose.

"Lenny I warned you that your path was a shitty one. Here we are in some hard working man's backyard waiting on my partner to come along so we can put the cuffs on you and haul you into jail." I am looking down at him while he tries to ignore my words, pretending to wipe away blood that is no longer there. "Not kiddy jail either. No. No more of that. We won't be taking you to your grandmother's or writing you a ticket this time either. When my partner gets here it's on with the cuffs and off to the prescient where you will be finger printed and booked; mug shots, jump suit, the whole deal."

"Whatever." He tries to sound like he doesn't care but if that were true he wouldn't have run away in the first place.

"Breaking into houses now Lenny? It didn't start out this bad, did it? I warned you."

He interrupts, "I didn't break into anyone's house, man."

"Oh really because we received a call about a breaking and entering and the suspect just happened to be your height, you're complexion, your hair color, and was wearing a big, red, bright ass coat. Not to mention that as soon as we approached you it was off to the races."

"Whatever," he says again. "It wasn't his house."

"How do you mean?"

"It was his garage. It wasn't even attached to his house." He seems satisfied with his answer; like it actually makes him right, or at least somehow less wrong.

"Oh, so if you don't keep your belongings in your house then they don't actually belong to you, is that it? If it's in your garage it's up for grabs? Sorry pal, that isn't how it works. You broke and entered a garage. It's the same crime as if you had broken and entered his home." He sure is a hard headed smart ass.

In a stunning exclamation of wit he retorts, "whatever," yet again.

"Whatever is all you keep saying, huh? I believe I recall you saying 'whatever' when I picked you up for stealing candy from Nowak's in the third grade." I stop and look at him and then look up as if I am struggling to recall something. "In fact you may have said 'whatever' when I picked you up in the fifth grade for stealing from Nowak's again, cigarettes I believe."

"I wasn't stealing. I had credit there with my grandma."

"Of course you did, that's why you ran both times. Not to mention that I doubt granny would be springing for cigarettes for her nine-year-old grandson. Or were you ten?"

"I don't remember."

"I don't remember how old you were either but I do remember something else. I remember telling you that you were heading down a dark path and that you better straighten out or someday I will be taking you to the big boy jail."

"Whatever man."

"Ah yes, 'whatever' again. I believe that is what you said to me when I came to your house because you through that rock through your girlfriend's window just a couple of years back."

"That was an accident."

"Sure it was. It was nice of your grandma to pay for it so you didn't have to spend any time in a juvenile facility. Wasn't that nice of her?"

"She's a real saint." He says this with extreme sarcasm being the ungrateful pain in the ass that he is.

"She has been trying to help you along but with your attitude I wouldn't expect you to ever show her any appreciation or to change your ways. At least you never decked her like you did your old man."

"He's not my old man!"

"Okay, well whoever he was he sure was upset when he called the police. He wanted you to go in for assault and harassment. I believe he had himself an argument too after seeing what you did to that man's eye. I recall that your mother convinced him that she would handle it."

This time he looks at me and seems ready to say, or possibly do, something. I am standing balanced while he is sitting in a sandbox with a busted nose so I am not too concerned.

I wait a long moment, in which he says nothing, and then continue, "I guess no one really handled it after all did they? That was a little less than a year ago wasn't it?"

He nods his head but says nothing and his eyes are burning at me.

"It's too bad that we couldn't have brought you in that night; it would have saved both of us from this jog through the neighborhood. Maybe it would have kept you from busting up your nose."

"He hit my mom." He says this quietly and looks to the ground when he says it.

"Then I guess you should have called us," I say this knowing that if some guy had punched my mom I would have done the same thing he did. That wouldn't have happened in my house though. My dad was home from his shift in the steel plant every day by five thirty. He never once struck my mom. He rarely laid his hands on my brothers or me either. The few times that he did we sure merited it.

"Whatever."

"You know Lenny this one's a big deal but you are only a kid. How old are you now?"

"Fourteen."

"Fourteen. Well like I said only a kid. I am sure that your grandmother will try and help, and she may be able to get you a good lawyer and make this better for you but this is a real big deal. She won't be able to erase it completely."

"Whatever."

"All right smart ass, stop saying 'whatever' and listen to me here. You're young and if you straighten up you can still have a good life ahead of you. By the time you turn eighteen and are ready for college this could all just look like youthful indiscretions. That is if it stops now." I stop and look at him. He is looking at the ground and tracing a circle with his finger in the sand but I think he might be listening. "However, if you don't learn from this then it's only going to get worse for you. If you don't believe me just take a look at yourself as an example." I look at him and take notice that he has stopped tracing in the sand. "Just six or seven years ago you were stealing candy and now you're stealing from houses."

"Garages," he reminds me. Well I guess he was listening, just not caring.

Now it's my turn, "Whatever."

We go back to waiting in silence for my partner. He saw where I went and I wonder what the hell is taking him so long to get back here. I suppose I could walk Lenny out to the street and find him but after our chase I don't feel like it. Plus, I wouldn't want Lenny to get another opportunity to take off on me. I grab my walkie and bark, "Where the hell are you Dick?"

"I'm in front of the house. Are you coming out or what?" Squawks back the old walkie-talkie.

"Damn it you lazy ass, get back here and cuff this kid for me." I chuckle knowing that he was probably just arriving here himself and that he was razzing me about waiting out front this whole time. After a chase the best part is seeing the perpetrator in defeat. It's not as gratifying when it's a kid though.

Realizing that he is just a kid prods me to give him one more talk over. "Listen, I mean it, you can still get your act together and make a decent time out of your childhood. You're almost done with the school year and still have all of high school in front of you. If not though, you're grandma won't be able to get you out of the trouble that you are heading for."

I am pleased that he doesn't give me a 'whatever.' I take it as a sign that he may be mulling it over. Our silence is interrupted by my partner Dick.

"Geez you're just a kid." Dick has only been my partner for a couple of months and hasn't yet had the pleasure of meeting my derelict friend Lenny until today.

"I'm fourteen," said with a twinge of defiance.

"That just proves my point." Dick looks at me with

that look that most police officers reserve for young criminals. It's both sadness for whatever has led this kid to this way of life and frustration at how many more times we are sure to deal with him in the upcoming years. It is one thing to arrest some middle aged junkie, it's easier to distance yourself from that. It's an entirely different thing to watch a child derail their life over a period of several years.

"Get him cuffed and down to the car while I go and let the owner of this house know that everything is under control."

Dick nods and starts toward Lenny while I walk towards the backdoor where I saw the husky man earlier. I stop and turn to Dick, "You know what Dick, just take him down and get him booked. I will stop and get a statement from the house that he burgled down the street and meet you at the coffee shop around the corner whenever you're done with him." This will give me a chance for a breather.

"You got it Ed."

"When he gets his phone call be sure to dial for him and make certain it's to his grandma. You better call ahead to Brian down at the precinct and let him know to get a juvenile cell ready." We can't have him sitting in a cell with all the big guys just yet.

As I am heading toward the house I hear Dick

telling Lenny, "You're in for a world of shit now kid. If there is anything Brian hates more than booking criminals it's booking punk kid criminals."

Although I am a pretty good distance away by the time Dick is finished I hear Lenny's response clearly.

"Whatever."

FIFTEEN

June 13, 1993

"What's up Mr. Walker?" I hear the voice and know that it's Leonard before I even look up from my desk. He has yet to enter through the door to my classroom. The door is in the back of the classroom while my desk is in the front. He is still in the hallway.

"How are you doing Leonard?" I ask him this as he enters my class.

"You tell me," he says this as he sits in the last seat of the room, putting as much distance between us as possible. He didn't always sit in the back of the class for me.

"How do you mean?" He is acting like he doesn't care because there are still many students in the hallway and he wants them to think that he doesn't. The buses have left but students tend to stick around at the end of the year to pick up final papers, play pickup basketball, clean out lockers, or smoke cigarettes across the street under the tree.

Year after year it's the same. These kids pretend

that they are so excited when the year ends but many of them are lost without the bells and are already looking forward to the structure of another year.

Leonard doesn't want anyone in the hall to think that he actually cares about school in any way so he slouches in his chair and looks away from me.

"Look Mr. Walker you were the one who asked me to come here." Leonard finally speaks after he feels that he has fully satisfied anyone in the hall who may be watching him.

"And?" I am not sure what I am looking for him to say next exactly but if I hear it I will know it.

"And, you told me that if I didn't show up I wouldn't have any chance of getting out of your class."

"And?" Again, I am looking for something. Something that will tell me this kid is worth all of my effort. Something that will confirm to me that my staying up at night devising ways to possibly reach this boy has been worthwhile.

"And I figured that I probably failed so you are going to tell me to get ready for another year. Or maybe tell me I have summer school or something? I don't know. Like I said you asked me here so why don't you just tell me how I am doing so I can bolt?"

"How do you think you did this year?"

"I failed every other stupid class so I probably failed this one too." He manages to slouch even further into his chair. He looks to be one more slouch away from possibly falling out of his chair.

I stand up and start to walk around the room in no particular pattern. I walk until I come to a wall or a desk and re-route my trip. The ultimate destination is the desk beside Leonard.

"So did I fail?" He interrupts my silent one-man motorcade.

"Leonard," I say while walking at him, "you haven't turned in even one final copy of any writing assignment that I have given you." I reach Leonard's desk, look at him, and continue, "You started the year as a quiet boy in the middle of my classroom." I point to the desk he began the year in. "It only took you a couple of weeks to make some acquaintances and move to the back of my room. There you and your acquaintances disrupted my class regularly."

"Look whatever," he says interrupting. "Mr. Walker, they are my friends and we just don't care about creative writing."

Now it is my turn to interrupt him. "They may not care about creative writing but you do. I know you do because you always turned in your pre-writing and sometimes you even turned in a rough draft. Leonard I know that you do because I have your free writing journal at my desk. I found it about a month ago on the floor. I read it. I read all of it and it is wonderful. You have an imaginative brain. You have a creative power that is impressive."

"Thanks." He says this with a tone of 'I don't give a shit' and hint of 'I don't care' but his eyes want more.

"Leonard I wish you would have turned in a final copy for an assignment or two."

"So you could give me an F?" His habit of interrupting me is starting to grate on my nerves.

"No, if you would let me finish you would have heard me say that I would have had something to read that truly compelled me to want more. I read your journal and want more. So I am curious as to how good your best can be."

"Really?" I've got him, he cares. I can see it in his face and hear it in his voice.

"Yes really. Your pre-writes and early drafts have been so promising but then you floundered around in the back with those acquaintances of yours and never finished even one paper for this class.

"Whatever, I hate school anyway. I especially hate creative writing." He says while looking down at the many juvenile words he has doodled onto his desk over the course of this year.

"Why?" I ask. "Because you can't spell? Because your handwriting is atrocious? Because you are scared?"

"Whatever?"

"Don't 'whatever' me. I don't care about your spelling or penmanship and I sure don't care about your run on sentences." I say this sternly and forcefully.

He looks at me with confusion on his face.

I continue, "I don't care about any of those things. I can teach you those things. However, I can't teach you how to grab a reader by the hand and lead him through the pages, eagerly jumping from one page to the next. I can't teach you how to bring a tear to someone's eye with gut wrenching heartbreak. I can't teach you how to wipe that tear away with a humorous quip. The good thing is that you already know how to do those things in a basic and unrefined way."

He looks at me with a look that I am not entirely familiar with but I believe that it may be a little bit of hope.

"Look Leonard I know that some of what you have written about in your journal is personal and the character names are just to hide your pain but I think you are an interesting person with an amazing story to tell."

The look of what may have been hope fades away and is replaced with anger. "Look Mr. Walker are you going to fail me or not? I want to get out of here; my friends are waiting for me."

"Leonard those aren't your friends. By definition I don't believe that they are friends to anyone. They don't care about you or even each other. They are acquaintances that will be around only as long as you are bringing something to the table for them; only as long as you continue to sully your reputation under that tree out there."

"Whatever. They are waiting for me so did I fail or not?"

"You can't fail me Leonard. You can only fail yourself." This may be a bit too dramatic but I am on the verge of losing him and have to try something, anything to get him back.

"How about this class Mr. Walker? Did I fail this class?"

"Leonard I am going to pass you from my class but I have already had you placed into my Creative Writing II class for next school year."

"Then I guess I will see you in class Mr. Walker. Have a great summer." He's already out of his little desk and heading toward the door.

"Now hold on a second Leonard." I say this and he actually stops and turns around. I was expecting him to at least slow down but I am a bit surprised that he has given me back his attention.

"Will any of your acquaintances be joining you on the soccer team next year?" I believe that part of the reason that he began the year so quiet and relatively behaved for me was because we had already spent the previous two weeks during the summer practicing for the soccer season.

"Uh, I don't think so Mr. Walker." Leonard says it as if I am a moron for asking and maybe I am.

"Well then I suppose it will just be you this summer?" I want a definitive answer. He has been dodging this question all year long. Ever since the season ended he has been getting into more and more trouble and been attending less and less off-season workouts. He hasn't been to any since just before Christmas.

"I don't think so Mr. Walker. I don't think soccer is really my thing anymore."

"Oh really? I thought soccer was definitely your thing. You had an extremely impressive freshman season. You even received a call up to the varsity squad for the playoffs." I happen to be both the junior varsity and the varsity coach.

"I guess it was my thing back then."

"But it's not your thing now?" He can make varsity full time next year. Soccer can definitely be his 'thing' and it may even help him to make some better friends. He is brash and abrasive on the field, which bothered the upper classmen on the team. He is highly skilled and possesses more natural talent than most of the players older than him, which also bothered those guys, but I think that if he comes out and plays hard he can really improve his image.

"I guess not," he says shrugging his shoulders.

"Look, I know that you had to play on the team because the judge made you agree to join a school activity but you had a great season. I mean you could have joined a simple club that only met once a month, like art club or something, but you chose soccer. I think that you made that choice because you enjoy soccer. I would love to see you at our summer preseason workouts starting next week Leonard."

"You're right Mr. Walker the judge made me play and since I haven't gotten in any trouble this year I am free to do whatever I want now." He seems a little smug.

"Leonard you haven't been arrested, that doesn't mean that you haven't been in any trouble." He seems to be forgetting all the afternoons that he has spent in detention. He doesn't seem to grasp that the fights he gets in here at school would be considered assault if they happened at the supermarket or in the mall.

"Whatever." This is an all too common response from Leonard.

"Okay, fine, whatever, but please don't leave before telling me what your 'thing' is these days?"

"What?" He is playing dumb, trying to give himself more time to think. I suppose I'll indulge him a little and elaborate.

"You said that soccer just isn't your 'thing' anymore. Well what is your 'thing' now?"

"Just being me." He seems outwardly satisfied with this answer but I want to know how that answer is sitting on the inside.

"Who is that?"

"What?" He seems uncomfortable.

"Being you, who is that? Who are you Leonard?" I am pushing at his lack of comfort and hoping that he will push back and find that he doesn't know who he is. I hope that he sees that with my help he might be able to find out a little bit about who he is. What high school freshman really knows who he is anyway? I certainly didn't.

"Look Mr. Walker I am a guy who is about to go and meet up with his friends."

"That isn't a good enough answer," I say while prodding for more.

"Well it is the one that will have to do for now because I am gone." He starts again for the door.

"Those guys will not help you figure out who you

are." He keeps walking. "They are not your friends." He stops and turns around just before exiting the room.

"You seem to know it all, don't you Mr. Walker." His eyes are piercing and his shoulders have squared up.

"Not everything."

"You don't know shit about me so back off and go grade some papers." His feet are set firm underneath him and his ears are turning red at the tips.

"I know more than you think I do Leonard."

"Okay, then why don't you tell me who the fuck I am. What's my thing?" I don't care for his tone or foul language at all but I think now is hardly the time to discuss it.

"Well Leonard since you have asked I feel obliged to tell you." I may regret this but I think he needs to hear it. "You are an under achieving, lazy, possibly depressed, young man looking for himself in all of the wrong places. As far as I can tell your 'thing' these days is getting stoned with your acquaintances who have already resigned themselves to a life of letting themselves and others down. Is that what you want for yourself Leonard? Do you want a life of letdowns and misery?" His face has faded to expressionless, except for his stabbing eyes, and he makes no movement as I am speaking.

We are staring at each other during this long pause

that has found its way in between the two of us. I am waiting for answers that I don't believe are coming. He is either waiting to see if I am finished with my assessment or he is trying to come up with a retort. I can tell that this interlude has drawn to an end when Leonard comes up with his fall back answer to anything that stumps or frightens him.

"Whatever." He turns to leave and this time I can tell he won't be stopped by anything that I have to say.

However, that doesn't stop me from saying, "You have plenty of potential Leonard," I also add, "and you're wasting it."

He's gone now and I have the entire summer to contemplate whether or not that was the right way to have handled everything.

SIXTEEN

November 16, 1994

"Now you keep your mouth closed up tight." I can hear her saying to the boy as they walk into my office.

I rise and greet them, "Good morning Mrs. Kingston."

"The snow is piling up and my grandson is facing the holidays in prison. How good a morning is it, sir?" She says while taking my outstretched hand. I am pleased that there is a desk between us.

"Some winter we are having, but I suppose that's the price we pay to live in Buffalo. As for your grandson's situation let's see what we can do about that." I look at the boy assuming that he will be the one in court.

I am pleased to see that although his crime is violent he, in appearance, is not frightening. This should help us with the judge. Sometimes these kids come in looking like gorillas and acting like them too. He is a smallish boy and looks to be about fourteen, although his file says he is sixteen coming up on seventeen. He is standing quietly and seems prepared to stay that way.

"Well your office is much nicer." She says this as if it was part of our ongoing conversation, yet I find that it doesn't fit.

"We have been here quite awhile now." I am unsure if she has been in my office before. It is by no means remarkable but it is decorated in the latest fashions and is near the top of the tallest building in Buffalo. It posses a grand view of the city.

"The other guy was near the mall." I realize that she must be talking about a former attorney. It is now that I remember that this case was transferred to me just recently and that we go to court early next week.

"Well I am sure that we will represent you and your interests much more appropriately than any counsel that is located outside of the city limits." Mall lawyers are nothing more than ambulance chasers and rarely have experience in anything outside of civil suits.

"My interests are having my grandson home for the holidays Mr. May." She is quite direct in her desires.

"Well let's have a seat and begin then shall we?"

She nods to me and says, "Sit down over there Leonard." There are two seats in front of my desk but only she sits down across from me. Leonard, as directed, takes a seat on the couch near the window overlooking the Queen City.

"It may be better if he has a seat here with us at the desk. I will be asking him some questions." I motion to the chair on her right.

"That won't be necessary today Mr. May." She apparently doesn't know how this generally goes. This could be why she is changing representation so close to the court date. "I will be answering your questions today."

"Well I don't think that will fly in court Mrs. Kingston." I am prepared to say more when I am interrupted.

"Well, Mr. May, we are not in court today. We are in your fine office overlooking the city of Buffalo. So, for today, I will be answering your questions."

"Yes, I see your point. However, I am going to need some information from Leonard directly seeing as he is the client." I am growing frustrated with her. We have very little time to prepare for this and she is already wasting my time. I get these kinds of clients from time to time. Parents, or grandparents, who can't see that there little 'Johnny' or 'Susie' could have possibly done anything wrong. They are quite hard to please.

"Mr. May I urge you to remember who is paying your fees. It isn't your client."

"Well then Mrs. Kingston, let us begin." I look at Leonard who looks to be detached from the whole ordeal and is gazing out of the window.

"Yes, let us indeed." This is going to be a long day.

"Well I see from Leonard's file that this is not his first incident with the police." He has quite the rap sheet for a boy of sixteen. He seems to be an accomplished little delinquent. Of course I can't word it like that to a lady like this.

Mrs. Kingston only nods to acknowledge my statement. She is trying to look like a proud and prominent lady rather than the caregiver to a derelict. Some guardians are open and allow me to ask questions freely but I can tell that Mrs. Kingston is not one of those guardians.

"Will Leonard's father or mother be at court with us?"

"No they will not." I have gathered that she isn't going to be forthcoming with information but this is like pulling teeth.

"Why is that?"

"I fail to see how that is either relevant or your business." Looks like I struck a nerve.

Here we go. "I, as Leonard's councel need to know everything about this boy and as much about his life as is possible. I need to know who will be at court, how they are related, and what kind of influences that they have on the boy. I need to know about his prior arrests and what the conditions surrounding them are. I need to have every resource available at my fingertips in case I see a weakness in the judge. Maybe he has a troubled grandson, maybe he was a troubled nephew, maybe he is from the same neighborhood, anything that I can use to sway him to allow your grandson to spend as little time behind bars as possible." I hope that my tangent has loosened her lips a little.

"Well then, if you must know?" She stops speaking and looks to me for more assurance that this is indeed necessary.

"I must." I keep a straight face and don't break eye contact so that she knows that I am serious. She may act like a 'somebody' but I know by her address and by her grandson that she is only a few steps above, and a few blocks over from, white trash.

"His father passed away years ago and his mother will be unavailable."

"Unavailable? How?" My questions are coming fast and hard in an attempt to leave no room for argument.

"She won't be able to attend."

"I gathered that already. Why not Mrs. Kingston?"

"She's gone." Leonard mumbles from the couch.

I immediately look in his direction hoping to get more information. When none comes with immediacy I prod, "Gone where?"

He shrugs his shoulders.

"That's enough from you Leonard. Please quiet down and wait for us to finish." This time Leonard doesn't look out the window. He continues to look at me.

"When was the last time that you saw her?" I ask Leonard.

"It's been some time." Mrs. Kingston answers.

"How long is 'some time' Mrs. Kingston?" I would rather direct my question to Leonard but his eyes are fixed again on the city.

"A few months," she says while looking down. Her pride has left her. Her eyes reflect someone who is less sure of herself than she were mere minutes ago. Her face seems older, more weathered.

"Years," comes another mumble from the couch. Eyes still fixated on the city below.

"Leonard that is enough! I will not tell you again." She doesn't quite shout this but it is a far cry from composed.

"Well, which is it months or years, Mrs. Kingston?"

"Years." This time the mumbling comes from her very own lips.

"How many years has it been since you have seen or heard from her?"

"We haven't seen her in nearly two years." She looks extremely nervous, almost as if she is hiding something. I press on.

"Now when was the last time that you heard from her?"

She doesn't answer. She doesn't even move. Leonard, on the other hand, has transferred his eyes from the city to his grandmother.

"Mrs. Kingston please answer the question. When was the last time that you spoke with Leonard's mother?"

"My daughter."

"When did she speak with your daughter?"

"No, Leonard's mother is my daughter."

"Thank you for clearing that up." I don't pause long before diving back in, "When was the last time that you spoke with your daughter?"

She looks away from me to find that Leonard's eyes are glued to her. From where I sit it appears that in his eyes are mixed measures of anxiety and wonder, sadness and hope, curiosity and fear.

"Just last week," she squeaks with a look of shame.

"What?" Her answer is enough for me but Leonard clearly wants more.

She doesn't say a word but in turn stares back at him.

"Is there some discrepancy here?" I am trying to help Leonard push as I decide that there may be something that Mrs. Kingston is holding back that I could be able to use in court.

Turning to face me Mrs. Kingston says, "Can we please do the rest of this conversation in private?"

Absolutely not. First she wants the boy in the corner and not to say a word, and now she wants him in the hallway or possibly even further away. How can I possibly get his side of things without him in the room? Of course I don't get to say any of this because Leonard answers her for me.

"No. I am not going anywhere until you tell me what is going on with my mom." He is standing now and making his way towards the desk.

"In light of all of this discussion I think that it is best for Leonard to join us here at the desk." I have felt this way all along but it seems that it will be happening in just a moment anyway and I would like everyone to know that it was my idea from the beginning.

"Yes, please join us Leonard," Mrs. Kingston says from a diminished position.

"What's going on with mom?" He takes a seat as

he finishes his question, although it comes out more like a demand.

"Listen Leonard, I need you to stay calm and listen carefully."

At this point I am merely along for the ride in this family discussion from wacky land.

"Just tell me," he demands.

"Your mother is in jail and has been for nearly two years." She says this pragmatically. She says this like I have told my wife that our electric bill has doubled during the winter. Yes it's a pain in the ass and yes it sucks but it wasn't entirely unexpected and now we just have to deal with it.

"What the fuck for?" Leonard clearly doesn't handle this situation as my wife handles the electric bill.

"Leonard!" A look of extreme surprise has taken over Mrs. Kingston's face.

"Okay, okay settle down." I say this and they both stop and look at me. I didn't expect such immediate attention but I continue, "I am no family psychologist but it is clear to me that we must figure out what is going on here before we can move on to our strategy for next week. I want you to sit back in your chair and allow your grandmother to explain."

Leonard shockingly takes the advice. I look at Mrs. Kingston and nod. I must admit that I am intrigued to see what is going on here. Much of what I have learned will undoubtedly help our situation in court. Sympathy really carries.

"Leonard's mother," I am surprised to see that she is speaking to me, "was arrested nearly two years ago for possession of narcotics." This is all she says and I am sure she is holding back information. No one gets two years for possession.

"What else?"

"She attacked the officer that was arresting her." She sounds exasperated. This still doesn't quite tell the whole story. To get two years for this she must be a repeat offender but I have no time to question further because Leonard has his own questions.

"When were you going to tell me?" Leonard is still sitting back in his chair and his voice is cool and measured. However, his eyes are infernos of pain and betrayal.

"I was hoping that I wouldn't ever have to." She goes on, "Your mother is cleaning up her act in jail and she is going to start over new when she gets out."

"When is that?" He is clearly scathing.

"Based on her behavior, she will be released in five or six months." I can tell that he is crushed by his body language. He looks as if he was kicked in the stomach.

"I hate to push all of this aside but we do have to

take a look at Leonard's case and what we can do about it."
This is a less than smooth attempt at a transition.

"Get him out of this so he can be home with us for the holidays Mr. May."

"It isn't that simple Mrs. Kingston. Leonard has prior arrests and is being charged with felonies."

"It was a simple misunderstanding Mr. May."

"Mrs. Kingston your grandson broke and entered a home and assaulted the man living there." She seems oblivious to the severity of the crimes in question. "How could this be a misunderstanding?"

"He was invited into the house. He goes to school with the boy who lives there."

"Leonard is this accurate?"

"You are speaking with me now Mr. May." She appears assured again, seemingly oblivious to the incidents that occurred just moments ago.

"I would really like his account of things Mrs. Kingston."

"I am giving you his account of things Mr. May. He was invited in by the boy and while he was there they had a disagreement and you know how it goes, boys being boys." I think that part of her actually believes that this may have essentially been what had happened.

"Mrs. Kingston that is not what the facts say."

"Oh really?" Is she trying to screw with me here? I don't have the time to be dicked around.

"Yes really. According to the police report he broke into this man's house. He was in the process of burglarizing it. When the owner of the house confronted him your grandson hit him in the head with…" I am interrupted.

"That can't all be true. Leonard was invited in by his friend; it wasn't as if this all happened in the middle of the night. Go and speak with the family and see what really happened." Mrs. Kingston is showing her hand. I can tell that she has no idea what really happened that night.

"I'm not going to speak with anyone. I am going to go with what the police report says because that is all that the judge will be going on."

"Well does the report mention Leonard's friend inviting him in after school?"

"Actually Mrs. Kingston according to the police report it happened around three o'clock in the morning." This quiets her so I proceed, "As I was saying, when the man confronted Leonard he struck him in the head with the blunt end of a screwdriver. It was that same screwdriver that he used to break the lock on the side door. He then repeatedly kicked the man until his son, who happens to go to the same school as your grandson, tackled him and held him down until the police arrived."

When I have finished summarizing the police report for her I look at her and she is silent. She looks as if this is the first time that she has heard the news, which can't be true because I am sure that the police would have relayed it to her as his guardian. She must have been aware of these charges when she posted bail. She also would have heard this same summarization from her previous mall lawyer.

"That's pretty much how it went," Leonard smirks. He seems demented. I think the news of his mother has affected him deeply. "I guess you can just throw me in jail with my mother." This comment and his devious leer confirm my suspicion.

"Be quiet Leonard. You don't know what you are saying."

"I know just what I am saying. I beat that man when I was robbing him and when I get back to school I'm going to beat on his son too."

"Quiet Leonard, don't say those things in front of your lawyer." She is on the verge of losing her cool again. Frazzled.

I don't want this to turn into one of those shows you see in the middle of the day with all the family members fighting and throwing chairs so I better say something. "It's okay Mrs. Kingston I am going to be looking out for his best interests. Anything he says to me won't be reaching the judges ears unless I deem it necessary. Please let him speak freely."

"You better not double cross us Mr. May." I am astounded that she has relinquished control of Leonard's conversation.

I waste no time and turn to Leonard, "What exactly happened that night Leonard?"

His eyes meet mine but they seem dull. That fire and anger and sadness and fear and anything else that was in there is gone. I look to Mrs. Kingston with pleading eyes.

"Go ahead Leonard. You can speak to Mr. May."

I turn my attention back to Leonard and find the same dreary eyes. Earlier I noticed how outrageously dark brown they were, almost blending into the pupil. Now they seem to have gone astonishingly grey.

"Leonard please, I am only trying to help you."

"If you really want to help me then you can send me to jail." He abruptly gets up tossing over his chair. I don't believe that it is intentional but he rose with such force that the chair tumbled backward to the floor.

"Leonard, please," is his grandmother's feeble attempt to calm him.

"I'll see you at home."

"We aren't finished here," I interject.

"Just wait in the car and I will be down shortly."

She is almost pleading with the young man.

"No. I'll see you later on, at home. I'm taking the bus." He is gone so quickly that I believe my receptionist hears the message more clearly than we do.

I stand and cross the room to close the door. I return to my seat and see that Mrs. Kingston has not stirred or changed her expression since I had moved.

"I apologize for him," and, "he has had a difficult day," are all that she musters after a few more frozen moments.

"I understand. We are almost finished here ourselves." After having seen all of this I have come up with my strategy for next week rather quickly.

"Wonderful. So you will have all of this sorted out for us and we can expect it to be settled by the holidays." This should have been said in the form of a question. However, it was not.

"Well I don't know about all of that. I am going to suggest that we keep him out of jail."

"Of course we will be keeping him out of jail Mr. May. He is just a boy."

I am not sure what she thinks is going to happen in court so I decide that I better give her a heads up.

"Mrs. Kingston I need you to understand that there is not an attorney in this state that could keep Leonard from some form of punishment. He has a record, several of his previous incidents involve violence, and he is much closer to being a man than a boy. Not to mention that these are very serious crimes that we are dealing with here. Felonies, Mrs. Kingston." I am not sure if any of this registers because her expression refuses to change while I run down the facts.

"So what are we going to do?" Stone faced.

"We have some angles that will work out for us. The first one is how baby faced he looks. I want you to be sure that he is dressed well and in clothes that fit. If you can afford a suit then please have him wear one. If not I insist that he wear a collard shirt, a tie, and slacks. Be sure that everything is cleaned and pressed."

She nods and says, "I'll try and find him a suit."

"Please do," I respond. "Next we will argue that his home life has been rough. Don't get me wrong, I have seen worse, but his childhood has been no picnic. We need to play that card to the judge."

"How so?" she seems nervous.

"Well, we need to make it seem as if he hasn't been given a fair deal and that with some help from the court he can be changed for the better."

"What exactly will you be saying to the judge Mr. May?"

"I'll let the judge know that his father died when he

was just a boy and that his mother has battled addiction all his life and is currently serving time because of those battles. I'll suggest that in lieu of jail time he spends time in a juvenile facility, of your choice, where he can receive counseling and some much needed structure." I can see that her face is twisting as I speak.

"Mr. May——" this time it is my turn to interrupt her.

"I know what you are wondering Mrs. Kingston and yes I will suggest to the judge that this all begin after the holiday season. I believe that I can convince the judge that you will be able to keep him out of trouble for the next few weeks while he spends the holiday season with what is left of his family."

"No."

"No what?"

"No, you can't say that."

"Which part?"

"Mr. May, I forbid you from discussing any of our family's gaffes in court." She seems firm in this request.

"Mrs. Kingston I don't see any other options here. Leonard is in serious trouble and this is the best that I can do." People seem to think that if you pay money for a lawyer that you will get out of the peril that you are in front of.

"Well I regret to inform you that we won't be using

your services next week."

"Regret is an interesting word to use there, Mrs. Kingston. I don't think that you realize how much you will regret heading to court next week without any representation for your grandson. Without a lawyer the court will immediately throw him into an over populated and understaffed state run juvenile facility. Or possibly even a penitentiary seeing that he is so close to the age of eighteen." I don't actually believe that they would put him in a real jail but some of those youth facilities aren't much better.

"I think that we will be better off on our own rather than letting you, or any other lawyer, throw our good name under the bus." Is she serious?

"Are you serious?"

"My fine husband, Walter, and I will be there and that should be enough for any judge with good sense to see that our boy will do fine left in our care. I am sure that we will impress the judge and he will leave our Leonard with us."

"Good luck."

"Good day!"

SEVENTEEN

September 18, 1995

"Please sit down Leonard." The guard has just brought me my next patient.

He is an interesting young man. By first appearances he is good looking and non-threatening. I would say that his young face makes him cute rather than handsome. He is small in stature and holds boyish features, which can disarm your worries when looking at him. That can be a dangerous thing to do in a place like this.

When I first observed him in his cell, quietly reading, I had to go back to my office and reread his file. I was surprised to see how often he was arrested, or at least questioned, for acts that were violent in nature. I was looking forward to our first session. This was several months ago. Now I only look forward to the hour being up when having to deal with Leonard Lamply Jr.

"I tell you every week, that is not my name anymore."

"And I remind you that while you are in this office I will refer to you by your name rather than your serial number Leonard."

"It's not Leonard anymore," he sings in an out of melodic way. "It's 2833256 now." His eyes narrow when he says this.

During our first session I noticed those eyes. Not at first. At first things were going fairly well but at some point his eyes narrowed and blazed with angst. I have gone over my notes from that first session time and time again but I can find no reason why his demeanor changed so quickly and dramatically. He has treated these sessions poorly ever since we were half way through that first hour.

I can only assume that he was afraid that I would get him to look at his emotions, his heartbreaks, his fears, and it scared him. A boy like this only has a handful of reactions when he is scared. I suppose that I am thankful that he did not turn violent. His eyes tell me all that I need to know about what kind of person he can become when he is angered.

"Leonard when you go back into the world what would you like people to call you?" I am attempting to ask questions that will prepare him to start thinking about his life on the outside of this facility. We only have a few months until his eighteenth birthday and have made very little progress.

Eventually we will have to talk about what his plans for work and housing are. I have to record this information, as well as any goals he may have, to give to the judge. However, today we can start with his name.

"I don't care!" This along with 'whatever' are popular responses from Leonard.

"That can't be true. I would be willing to surmise that you have been in arguments or even fights because people called you names that you didn't like being called." I give him a look that tells him that I know that I am right and that he needs to come up with a better answer.

"I guess you're right." He flashes a wicked grin telling me that I was correct but that I can't fully grasp to what extent.

"So then what would you like people to call you in a few months?"

"Four," he says forcefully. I believe that I am safe in assuming that the force is generated from the thoughts of things he's done in the past due to being called atrocious names at home and in the school yard.

"Four?" I don't think he is answering my question but I can't be sure; maybe 'Four' is what he would like to be called.

"Actually, four months and five days to be exact

Doc." I realize that he is talking about his release date.

"That is the day of your eighteenth birthday Leonard."

"I don't care about my birthday. That is the day that I will get out of this shit hole."

"You are correct but if you get into anymore trouble your release will be revoked and you will be sent to a real prison Leonard."

"Not that I would do anything wrong, but even if I did I wouldn't be getting caught again that's for sure."

"What would make you say that?" Before he can answer I squeeze my point of view in, "You will be on probation which will force you to see an officer once a week. He will need to see your documentation of work and he will administer drug tests monthly. Also, you will be seeing a psychiatrist once a week who will be reporting directly to that officer. Of course they won't be able to tell the officer anything that you confer together but they will be able to discuss your progress, or lack thereof."

"Whatever."

"You have managed to get us off topic for the better part of five minutes Leonard. Let's get back to my question please."

"What was that question again Doc?" I know that he remembers. He, as usual, is doing anything he can to make the hour go by without actually telling me anything.

"I asked you what you would like to be called when you are out of this facility."

"You mean instead of 2833256?" He gives me another smile, but this one seems more playful rather than devious. I could be wrong but I don't think that I am.

"Yes, I do." I test the waters and give him a smile of my own.

"I wouldn't mind being called Mr. Lamply." He looks down as he answers. He seems as if he is embarrassed to give an answer.

"Like a teacher?"

"I don't like teachers." He sounds like he is forcing himself to say that, like it is rote.

"You don't like teachers?"

"Nope." He doesn't sound sure.

"But you want to be called Mr. Lamply?"

"Yep." Of this he sounds sure.

"There has never been a teacher that you liked? Not one?" I can feel he wants to let me in. He doesn't want to let me in on many topics, like his dad, his mom, basically any family member, or his living in so many different places before he eventually ended up at his grandparent's house. These things seem to be shut in pretty tight; too tight to be reached once a week in one meager hour. However, I can feel that on this thing he wants to let me in.

"Maybe one or two weren't so bad?" This is it I'm getting in! I must temper my excitement so I don't scare him back off.

"Do you remember their names?"

He merely shrugs his shoulders. Other than that one false act his body language is begging me to continue.

"How about grades?"

"I never got good grades." He is a smart ass but I don't care because I can tell that he will give me more if I work for it a little.

"I don't think that is because you aren't capable. I think you are a very smart young man. However, I was referring to what grade you were in when you liked one of your teachers?"

He knows that is what I had meant but I don't mind a little back and forth after so many sessions of silence. So many of these young men that come in here just sit silently in my office for the entire hour, it can be rather boring. It so happens that the young man that was in here prior to Leonard was one of these mute cases.

"I don't really remember." We both know that this isn't true. "I think it might have been first grade." He pauses. "Yeah it was first."

"What was your teacher's name that year?"

"I don't remember." I know he is bluffing.

"Try a little harder." I am aware that I seem overly eager.

"Sorry I can't remember," he smiles and winks his left eye making me more than aware that he too is aware of my zeal.

"That's okay. Why did you like her?"

"She let us take naps at our desk."

"Wow that is special. I thought nap time ended in kindergarten." Come on, tell me more.

"They did but she would let you put your head down and sleep if you wanted to." He is smiling as he recollects those days in his first grade classroom.

"Why were you so tired in school?"

"I wasn't tired," he catches on immediately to what I am digging for, "I just hated learning that's all."

"Was there anything else you liked about that class in first grade?" I am hoping that he hasn't shut down on me.

He hesitates for a moment then says, "No, that teacher was probably a pervert anyway."

"What makes you say that?" This has taken quite a twist.

"She was always hugging us and she used to kiss my cheek a lot." He fakes an expression of disgust, but I can tell by his eyes that he enjoyed that gentle attention from his teacher. Leonard often uses his eyes to scare off people by showing how he is feeling on the inside, which is generally anger, but in this instance those eyes have betrayed him.

"Can you remember any other teachers or grades that you enjoyed?"

"Nope." Just like that he is shut off again. Cold.

"Okay. Well Mr. Lamply, what would you like to do when you are released?"

"I want to get a bucket of fried chicken with a side of mashed potatoes and gravy. The food in here blows."

"You are not the first person I have heard with that complaint. I was wondering rather, what kind of work you would like to do when you are released. How will you make a living?"

"I don't know." He spouts this as if I am the lunatic for asking.

"Well if you want to be called Mr. Lamply you will have to figure out something. To get the 'Mr.' you are going to have to be in charge of something."

"In charge?"

"Yes. Like how a teacher is in charge of the classroom. A foreman is in charge of the construction site. A 'Mr." has a staff or a group of people that he is in charge of. You will have to be in charge of something Mr. Lamply."

"I don't know, maybe I will be a teacher." I had a feeling we would be back here. This is the only place that he has let me in and now he has brought me back here so quickly. I have to try and figure out why.

"I think that you would make a fine teacher Leonard."

Rather than correct me about his name being some series of numbers, he smiles. "What would I teach?"

"What do you like?"

"Nothing."

"That can't be true, everybody likes something."

He shrugs his shoulders and says nothing.

"Well I suppose that we can figure out what you like some other time. For now let's stick with what you are going to do when you get out of here, after you get your chicken of course."

"Whatever." He doesn't use the word to object. It is almost as if he is cueing me to say 'go on doctor, I'm listening' or something to that effect.

"To be a teacher you are going to have to get back into school. You will have to finish high school and probably take some college courses. If you take your studies a little more seriously I think that you can be almost caught up to your senior year before you are released."

"Screw that."

"Screw what?"

"Being a teacher, going to school, any of that shit."
He is getting indignant. I hope that I can redirect him
before he goes over the edge and the remainder of the
session is lost.

"Well then what do you want to do Leonard? You
have to want to do something, enjoy something, yearn for
something." I am growing a little frustrated myself and
need to calm down. It is so agitating to have been finally
making some progress with this young man and then to
watch him shut down again.

"Start a band." I am not sure if he is pulling my leg
or not. I don't care; I am going to treat this as an authentic
answer.

"What instrument do you play?"

"I don't."

"Then you will be the singer?"

"No." His answers don't seem to bother him. He
doesn't seem to see the problem with him being in a band
yet not knowing how to play any instruments and refusing to
sing.

"I don't know if I would want to come to your
concert if you don't play any instruments or sing Leonard."

"I don't play any instruments yet. I'm going to
learn to play the drums." He seems sure of this. I am glad

that I treated his dream as such. It seems his lights are back on and he is letting me in again. This is shaping up to be a very exciting session; one that in many ways validates my work here at the facility both personally and professionally.

"I think that is a wonderful idea Leonard. Do you know how you are going to learn that skill yet?" I want him to know that I believe in his dream while showing him that dreams are not easily attained. They take some work on behalf of the dreamer.

"Take lessons I guess?" He shrugs his shoulders and gives the impression that he believes that this will be easily achieved.

"You know Leonard; if your grandparents do take you back in, then you won't have to work. If you don't have to work then you could start taking steps toward this dream of yours."

"What do you mean? I thought one of my conditions was to work a job?" I have him. He is asking me a question. I have him!

Trying not to display my extreme joy in answering a question of his I calmly state, "There are a few ways around that."

"What ways? How?"

"Well, if you have a safe place to stay, like at your grandparent's, and are taking some other actions you can avoid working." I am being coy because if I rush into telling him that he needs to be back in school then I think he will quickly accept having to work instead.

"I can stay with my grandparents. There is no doubt about that."

"Are you sure?" From what I have read in his file I am sure that they will take him in myself, but I want to keep up this dialogue.

"Yes, I am sure. Now what else do I have to do?"

"Well if you are enrolled in a full course load you can avoid working." I inspect his face and he appears as if he may be contemplating this briefly.

"I think I'll just go to work Doc."

"Now hold on. I know what you're thinking."

"No you don't"

"I think I do. I think you don't want to go back to high school. I am thinking that you don't want to take anymore classes with assholes from high school." I don't normally use that kind of language but I am no longer in control. My exhilaration has taken over and I will say whatever is necessary to push Leonard into his dream. In the span of twenty minutes he has become my most important patient.

"Whatever."

"Now just hear me out before you give up so quickly

Leonard. You can take classes through a program that will give you a simple test at the end. It's called a Graduate Record Examination. If you pass that test you will be awarded the equivalent of a high school diploma." I look at Leonard with hope in my eyes and I think I see a speck of it in his as well.

"Do they teach drums?" He asks ever so hopeful.

"No." I pause so I can gather my next mouthful.

"So why the hell would I go to this place and take a test? I want to play the drums in a band Doc. I don't need a diploma to play in a band."

"You are absolutely correct about that but you do need a diploma to get into a community college." I can see that he is about to interject so I quickly persist, "At community college you can take just four classes and be considered full time. This full time status will enable you to forgo having to get a job, provided you can stay with your grandparent's."

"I already told you that I can stay with them Doc. What you haven't told me is why I would want to go to some crummy ass college?" I can tell that he is aware that I am leading him somewhere but that he is starting to get frustrated with the process.

"Leonard, you can take any four classes a semester that you like. They have all kinds of classes."

"I hate classes." He never misses an opportunity to jump in.

"Yes you have already told me that but you can take any classes that you want Leonard. While they do offer the more traditional English, Math, and History credits, they also have some courses you may like."

"Like what?" I am so pleased that he is interested that I smile, both outwardly and inwardly, before going on.

"Like in mechanical engineering which is just a fancy way of saying they'll show you how to soup up your car. Like in sports physics which is just a fancy way of saying they'll show you how to shoot a three pointer or kick a bender from thirty feet out. Like in musical instruction which is just a fancy way of saying that they'll show…"

"…me how to play the drums," Leonard finishes my sentence for me. He momentarily shows me a face full of delight but quickly hides behind indifference. "Maybe I'll look into that."

I am about to query further regarding how 'into it' he would be willing to look when I hear a knock on my door.

The door opens before I have a chance to inquire as to who is behind the door, revealing the guard who had dropped Leonard off a short time ago. He is monopolizing the doorway. He is an imposing man taking up most of the space that the door had just moments ago spoken for. This man must be over six feet tall and weigh upwards of two hundred and fifty pounds. It appears as if he doesn't miss a meal or a workout. He often brings me my patients and returns them when we are done. At times he seems to be a little overaggressive but, as it was explained to me, he can't be too careful because I am often the only woman that these young men see, aside from their mothers and sisters during visitations.

"Excuse me officer but we still have over twenty minutes remaining." I need him to leave immediately before he impedes all progress.

"My apologies doctor but we need fifty six back." He does this with all of the patients when they are in his charge. He refers to them by the last two digits of their facility number. There are far more young men in this facility than his short hand allows for but that doesn't stop him from using his two-digit system of acknowledgment.

"Please give us our twenty minutes and then he is yours for the better part of a week, until our next hour."

"Sorry Doctor but I can't do that." He says this to me. Then to Leonard he commands, "Stand up fifty six."

"Not a chance, Big Chocolate." This is what many of the young men call him. "We aren't done in here, now get lost."

"Why do you need him now?" I ask as he moves briskly toward Leonard.

"Contraband." He replies as he stands Leonard up and places handcuffs on the hands he apparently forced behind Leonard's back so quickly that I didn't even notice.

"You can't do that! You can't go in my cell without me!" Leonard is shouting.

I am trying to speak over Leonard, to the officer but he is already answering Leonard.

"You aren't staying at the Ritz fifty six. We can toss a cell whenever the fuck we want. Now shut up before I shut you up."

I am not sure what surprises me more; the way that the guard speaks to Leonard or the fact that Leonard listens. I don't waste much time pondering this as they are heading towards the door and I still want to speak with the both of them.

I start with the guard, "What did you find?"

"I can't discuss that with you right now Doctor."

"That's not accurate Officer. I am his Doctor and should be made aware of all developments in this young man's status while in this facility." I look to Leonard hoping that he sees me sticking up for his interests. I am hoping that this will enable us to be able to continue with any of the gains that we have made here today. Unfortunately his face is telling me that he has shut off. He has gone somewhere deep within himself.

"Sorry Doctor but now is not the time for this discussion." Only his words are polite.

I turn my attention to Leonard although he looks the same as he did a moment ago.

"Leonard, just think about all that we have accomplished here today. When I see you next time I will have a course catalog for the community college. I'll highlight some courses that I think you will like." He is out into the hallway and I don't expect him to reply because his eyes look to be so far away from this place.

His eyes, without warning, come back to his face as he thunders, "You can stick that catalog wherever they stuck my contraband. It's probably here, up in Big Chocolate's ass."

EIGHTEEN

January 23, 1996

"Good morning your honor," says a young lawyer whose name I cannot recall. I only see him occasionally as this is not his usual arena. Great, I get to start the morning with a juvenile case. I know that the dockets are full throughout the system but these sorts of hearings aren't meant to be heard by a judge of my standing.

"Let's get over the pleasantries and hurry along with this case. There are serious matters ahead of me today."

"I understand your honor, however I assure you that to the people gathered here today this is an extremely serious matter." Here we go. This little runt has been a lawyer for no more than a year and a half and he is going to explain how this court operates to me?

"What's your name?"

After frowning he gets on, "Moonan, James Moonan your honor."

After smiling at the young man I say, "Mr. Moonan I suggest that we precede with this important matter of yours immediately."

"Yes, thank you Judge Thompson for hearing us today." I am not sure if he realizes that I have no choice in the matter or if he is just being polite.

"Let's hear your argument for why this boy should be released." From the file that I have read this boy is heading for more trouble, and fast, but that won't stop me from releasing him. Today is his eighteenth birthday and if I don't release him then I will have to make arrangements for him to be transferred to an adult facility. Those spaces will be needed for the many cases that I will be hearing after this light workout.

I need to save those spaces for the armed robbers, rapists, and murderers. Judging by this Lamply's file I am sure that he will fill his space sooner or later. My hope is later but my gut says sooner.

"Yes, your honor. Leonard here has been in the custody of the state juvenile facility since just prior to his seventeenth birthday. He has complied with all of the stipulations set forth by the state and is seeking an unconditional release back to his family, who is gathered here today."

"I hardly believe that Mr. Lamply is deserving of an

unconditional release Mr. Thompson." I know that I am in a hurry but there is no way that I am going to release this punk unconditionally back into society.

"He has complied with all guidelines set forth your honor."

I must interrupt, "Hardly Mr. Moonan. He was in a physical altercation with another boy, two years his junior I might add, scarcely two months ago."

"That was an isolated incident based on a misunderstanding." I believe that this prick thinks that just because I am in a hurry that I am going to wash my hands of this. I might have been inclined to do so only several minutes ago but I don't take to anyone resting on me.

"Mr. Moonan! Are you telling me that you believe this boy to be fully rehabilitated and prepared for total adjustment to a regular, crime free, way of life? Is that what I hear you arguing?" That should remind him that he is in my courtroom, not the other way around. He better wake his ass up.

"I believe that any adjustments in transitioning out of incarceration that Leonard may face can be aided by his grandparents, who are here today. They care for him and are committed to his well being."

"According to his file he has been in two altercations with fellow inmates, beside the one that I have previously mentioned, and been caught on several occasions with contraband ranging from pornographic images to tobacco."

"Your honor!"

"I am not finished Mr. Moonan." Try to cut me off, does he? "According to his doctor he has made little to no progress in his emotional rehabilitation. He can be described as hostile, angry, and resentful."

"Your honor?"

"I am still not finished Mr. Moonan!" Maybe I can find some room upstate for his client after all. "Now after hearing this entirety do you still believe that your client should be released without condition?"

"I suppose some mandated counseling would be appropriate."

"I would say 'necessary' rather than 'appropriate' Mr. Moonan. Is that all Mr. Moonan? Do you think there are any other conditions that would help society protect itself from this young man?"

"It would behoove him to see an officer once a month." Just once a month, this guy is ridiculous.

"I believe it would behoove society to have this boy meeting with an officer once a week and adhering to random drug testing. Now, Mr. Moonan I am very close to releasing this boy under those conditions, but I must admit that I still have some trepidation about the consequences of doing so to society. Is there any other condition that you can think of that will help ease my mind?" I hope that it has become crystal clear to Mr. Moonan that just because this is not my usual case it does not mean I am baffled by it in any way.

"Not at this time your honor." He is a true nitwit.

"Then by all means, let me help you Mr. Moonan. I will release this young man under the following conditions: that he stay away from any law breaking in all forms, attend counseling once a week, visit a parole officer once a week, pass a minimum of one random drug test a month, and maintain fulltime employment. All of these conditions will last for one year. If at the end of this time Mr. Lamply has complied with each condition he will then be released from probationary status and will no longer have to comply with any of these conditions except for the first one."

"I assume that full time enrollment in school will suffice for full time employment?"

"You assume wrong Mr. Moonan." You know what they say about assumptions.

"Excuse me your honor?"

"Mr. Lamply is eighteen years old. He will maintain fulltime employment. That will leave him several hours remaining in the day to attend any classes, which he deems necessary for his advancement in the world. The busier that this young man is the better chances he will have of staying out of precarious situations."

"It is customary in these situations to grant allowances for education your honor."

"How long have you been working in these courts son?" This boy is still wet behind the ears.

"It is approaching two years your honor."

"That is hardly long enough to have any idea of what is 'customary' around here." I am about through with Mr. Moonan.

"Noted your honor."

"Maybe you should write it down so you don't forget Mr. Moonan. Now I would like to speak to Mr. Lamply." Mr. Moonan nudges the young man and he stands up.

He stands there awkwardly until Mr. Moonan leans over and whispers in his ear. Only then does he say, "Good morning sir."

"Young man, you have been in quite a bit of trouble in your short time here on this earth. I hope for your sake that it stops now. You have some family members here that I am sure you have been largely a disappointment to. I hope for their sake that it stops now. This is it for you son. You have run out of chances. The next step for you is the big house. Are we clear?"

"Yes sir."

I nod and crack the gavel. It is time for me to move on to the next of many cases.

Please direct any comments, criticisms, or inquiries to: leonardlamplyjr@gmail.com

Acknowledgements

I want to first thank God for all of the experiences that have made me who I am. I appreciate the humor. Thank you.

I want to thank my beautiful and supportive wife. Thank you for providing me with the time to write this book and the encouragement to keep going when the process became tedious. Thank you for participating in all of my madcap ideas.

Thank you to my three lovely daughters for your unconditional love and for showing me how fun life can be!

Thank you to my mother for providing me with the ego to think that I could pull this thing off. You are a wonderful mom.

I owe a big thank you to my brothers. Cully your positive feedback and constant backing in everything that I do keeps me going. Luke without the times that we have shared many of the stories in this book could never have been conjured. Dustin I thank you for watching out for the three of us knuckleheads down here.

Thank you to all of my friends and family who have read this book in any of its many forms prior to this point. Your feedback and cheer was highly appreciated and sorely needed.

This book is dedicated to Colleen Cotter. I love you and I miss you. Thank you for always believing in me.

Made in the USA
San Bernardino, CA
14 July 2014